D0271610

A STATE OF INDEPENDENCE

By the same author
THE FINAL PASSAGE

ff

CARYL PHILLIPS

A State of Independence

faber and faber
LONDON · BOSTON

First published in 1986
by Faber and Faber Limited
3 Queen Square London WC1N 3AU

Photoset by Wilmaset Birkenhead
Printed in Great Britain by
Butler & Tanner Ltd Frome Somerset

British Library Cataloguing in Publication Data

Phillips, Caryl
A state of independence.
I. Title
823'.914[F] PR6066.H45/
ISBN 0–571–13910–8

It is only a jellyfish that comes into the world and passes off without anybody knowing it was here . . . make St Kitts your Garden of Eden. If you don't do it other men will do it for you. Your country can be no greater than yourselves . . .

Marcus Garvey (Mutual Improvement Society Hall, St Kitts, 2 November 1937)

He was so drunk in Antigua that he tried to board the wrong flight. He was so drunk when he returned here that he did not know where he was taken. He was so knocked out with liquor that he vomited like a whale, urinated like a dog, exposed himself like a jackass, and wallowed in his muck like a pig.

St Kitts' government newspaper *The Democrat* – view of the leader of the opposition (1982)

Six more days for PAM. Six more days for the first ever jackass Prime Minister in the world, for scavenger Powell, for rubbernose Morris and for the rest of that corrupt gang of vampires who have been sucking the life-blood of the people of St Kitts for the past four and a half years.

St Kitts' opposition newspaper *The Labour Spokesman* – view of the government a week before the 1984 general election

Well, what you must realize is that we living State-side now. We living under the eagle and maybe you don't think that is so good but your England never do us a damn thing except take, take, take.

The Hon. Minister Jackson Clayton

It was twenty years since Bertram Francis had last seen the island of his birth. He leaned anxiously towards the window and tried to look through his neighbour. The woman was sleeping at an angle so awkward that Bertram felt as though he was peering through a climbing frame. She slept with her mouth open, which meant she snored, but the drone of the plane's engines ensured that nobody else could hear, even when she occasionally turned and her snore became a series of quick, low grunts. Bertram looked at her round, rather plump face. As she pulled in her chin, a second one formed and created a staircase that he felt sure many a tongue had slithered up. It was curious, thought Bertram, because from the neck down the rest of her body seemed both slender and firm. He imagined that some might mistake her for a woman ten years her junior, and that this would be her first time in the Caribbean, for in her lap she cradled a new, but already well-thumbed, guide to the area. Her flouting of regional ignorance somehow made him feel a little easier at the end of what had been a worrisome flight. He felt grateful that she was not a regular visitor who might have taken it upon herself to educate him about his own country and further disturb the feelings of guilt that lay inside him.

Almost imperceptibly the tone of the plane's engines

changed. Then the aircraft began to bank to one side, and despite the scaffolding of his neighbour's arms and legs Bertram saw sunlight bleeding through the clouds as they passed over the shoulders of the island. Below him lay a dense carpet of green forest, thin pools of mist entangled in the highest branches of the trees. And in a clearing he saw the crumbling stones and wild fern clusters of a disused sugar mill and broken-down Great House. They passed over a village whose corrugated iron roofs overlapped like the scales of a fish, and in the distance, beyond the village, Bertram saw the capital. He knew full well that from this height what appeared to be a neat and tropical Versailles would seem little more than a sprawling mess when on the ground. The plane began to bank to the other side, and Bertram now surveyed the shock-inducing blue of the Caribbean sea. The waves broke over the turquoise coral, and the people swam with only their severed heads visible. Then the plane lurched as it lost altitude, and Bertram's eyes closed as he imagined the long grey carpet unfolding beneath them.

The airport was small, though bigger than Bertram had expected. He had left by boat, for in those days the airport had been little more than a wooden shack in a canefield, the runway a curved gash someone had opened up with the blunt edge of a knife. Bertram remembered the first time he ever saw a plane land on the island, and how the entire classroom had stopped what they were doing and looked up in disbelief. Like a giant insect it whirred and circled overhead, then disappeared in the direction of a distant field. Everybody turned their attention back to the lesson, but each decided that after school they would try to be the first to see the plane close up. However, at the end of the day, Bertram's best friend, Jackson Clayton, announced that it was nothing but a piece of clumsy machinery. Bertram felt compelled to agree with him, and together they turned in the direction of home. It was not until some weeks later, when landings became more regular, and Jackson was at cricket practice, that Bertram was furtively able to view the plane (although he never admitted this small deception to his friend).

Now Bertram received priority disembarkation over those passengers merely in transit to one of the bigger islands to the south. He stepped down on to the apron and looked up at the mountains which posed as though in a family group. Above them the clouds drifted, crimson fortresses at peace. As the plane's engines died, the cicada-riddled hush of a late afternoon in the Caribbean overtook him.

The airport lounge was supported by clean white concrete pillars, each punctuated with round glassless holes. This helped the air to circulate freely, but the claustrophobia of the heat surprised Bertram. Not wishing to take off his jacket, Bertram concentrated on the signs that decorated the wall behind the desk of the immigration officer. Then he felt the first few drops of perspiration dribble from his armpits, catch the edge of his ribcage, and roll cold and wet towards his waist.

Welcome to Rum'n'Sun

And beneath this sign hung a second, and more assertive, placard.

INDEPENDENCE
Forward ever – Backward never

A blackboard and easel stood to the side of the desk. Someone had rubbed out a '4' and replaced it with a '3', so the message now read:

PROUD, DIGNIFIED AND BLACK!
NONE CAN TAKE MY FREEDOM BACK!
Independence soon come – only 3 days more

The immigration officer seemed uninterested in anything. Like the other people who worked in the airport, his skin shone as though he had spent the day occupied with stressful manual labour. Bertram looked at him, the young man's face seemingly vacant and uncluttered with thought, and wondered if he might be the victim of some form of lethargy-inducing sickness. He opened Bertram's passport, using the back of his palm to keep it flat, then glanced at the photograph, then up at Bertram, then back at the photograph.

'How long you planning on staying here?'

Bertram laughed, trying to remove some of the formality.

'I don't know, man. Maybe I come back to live.'

'Alone?'

'Alone,' said Bertram.

'You planning on working here to support yourself?'

'I look like a millionaire?'

The immigration officer stared blankly at Bertram, who now realized he would have to elaborate.

'Well, I don't know as yet. It depends on how things go.'

The man stamped the passport, flicked it back shut, and silently handed it to Bertram. As he turned to leave Bertram heard the man speak once more.

'Welcome home, Mr Francis.'

Bertram turned back to face him, but the young man was already attending to the next person in the queue. It was a severely-attired elderly woman. In the silence behind the mask of her face Bertram could tell she was a true national who had probably been to England only to see grandchildren. The speed with which she followed him down the steps towards the baggage reclaim section only served to confirm this in his mind for, unlike his, hers was a home-coming hastened by familiarity.

Bertram's two suitcases were waiting for him. He lifted them up on to the counter with other suitcases and boxes and parcels, whose battered states bore testament to much international scale-wrestling. The customs man looked at Bertram's luggage, but like his colleague at immigration he too seemed tired and indifferent. He enquired half-heartedly whether Bertram had anything to declare. Bertram shook his head. A huge cross was chalked on the side of both suitcases, and a brisk wave of the hand meant they were to be taken away.

'You need some help, man?'

A stocky, greying man in a sweat-stained shirt stood before Bertram. His trousers hung hopelessly at the crotch and were fat with turn-ups around the ankles.

'No, I can carry them alright.'

'You sure you can manage?'

The man backed out of the customs hall, and Bertram stepped forward into the open air and stopped. He put down the suitcases and glanced at the hills in the distance, small white houses dotted up and around the backs of these gentle green giants. The stillness of the sea in the foreground looked, at this time of the day, like a mirror set ablaze. To his left the few people who waited by the arrivals gate stood and shielded their eyes from the now dying sun. They stared with interest at those who trickled through, wondering if they resembled half-forgotten relatives. Then they stared with dismissal, almost contempt, when it became clear they did not.

'Well, a taxi then? I can arrange one for you.'

'I need to get to Sandy Bay.'

'Well, that's no problem, man. You just wait here while I bring round the car.'

The man limped, Bertram could now see that one leg was shorter than the other, across the grass verge and down to the tarmacked compound where he would collect his car. Bertram's eyes followed him, then he turned his attention to the poster that was pasted against the wall of the airport building. Peeling, and likely to flake apart at any moment, it advertised the forthcoming independence, and although the sun had sucked most of the ink from the paper much of it was still visible. If the man had not arrived with the taxi Bertram would have detached himself from the suitcases and gone across to take a closer look.

The taxi was a dark green Ford Corsair, a make of car Bertram had not seen for at least ten years. They were popular when he first arrived in England, but had rapidly become a joke car. Back on his home island the car seemed laughable to him, but the carefully-polished exterior, and the reverence with which his self-appointed driver parked it, then waddled around to collect the luggage, made Bertram aware that in this society, such a car was still a symbol of some status.

The man loaded the suitcases with a well-practised ease. As he did so Bertram noticed the knuckles of his hands were little more than bruised knobs, as though he had been the victim of some medieval torture. Clearly, driving a taxi had not been his only vocation.

'So where it is you say you need to get to?'

'Sandy Bay,' said Bertram. 'You know where the Francis house is?'

The taxi driver pushed back his peaked cap and scratched his grey and wiry hair.

'The Francis house,' he paused. 'No, man, I don't seem to be able to place it.'

'Well then, you just drive, and I going let you know as we get close to it.'

'You want me to drive to Sandy Bay?' asked the man.

'You didn't hear me? Or maybe Sandy Bay done slide into the sea since I left.'

'It's not going cost you soft, you know. Gas don't be cheap. And the Government putting a tax on spare parts so I must charge you thirty dollars. If it isn't for the Government I let you take the trip for twenty, but they squeezing everyone these days.'

Bertram quickly calculated that thirty dollars came to about eleven pounds. The alternative to taking the taxi was to wait for a bus, or to try and hitch a lift, but he had no idea whether a bus came to the airport, and there was nobody around whom he recognized.

'Thirty dollars seems alright to me,' said Bertram.

He looked at the taxi driver, who replaced his hat and began to nod slowly as if to say, 'Yes, Bertram, I agree with you, thirty dollars is alright.'

Bertram opened the rear door and slid across into the seat. Before slamming the door he called impatiently to the driver:

'Well, you going stand there all day?'

The man looked at him, then checked the boot was properly shut. He came around to the driver's side, opened his door, then got in and started up the engine. The car jumped forward, the man obviously having some trouble with the clutch, then it began to ease its way smoothly down the hill towards the main road, Island Road. They turned left and joined the thin line of traffic streaming away from the capital and into the country.

'So tell me,' said the driver, 'how long it is since you been away?'

'Twenty years,' replied Bertram.

Bertram noticed a roll of fat which bulged over the man's shirt collar.

'Well, one thing you going have to remember', said the driver, 'is that we don't rush things here. You rushing me too much, and I don't like to be rushed.'

Bertram was slightly taken aback by the brashness of the voice. Then he noticed the man now looking back at him in the rearview mirror, so he sat forward in his seat.

'Listen, I'm only trying to rush you for I'm not sure if you're hearing what I'm saying to you.'

'I know,' said the man, not bothering to turn around. 'I know why you're trying to rush me, but remember you're back home now and things do move differently here. I'm often picking up fellars who been living in England and America and all them places, and they coming back here like we must adjust to their pace rather than it's they who must remember just who it is they dealing with once they reach back.'

'I know who it is I'm dealing with,' said Bertram.

'Good,' said the man, 'for I don't be trying to make you feel bad. I'm just trying to help straighten you out.'

Bertram sat back in his seat and looked out of the window. The man turned on the crackly radio and tuned it into the local station ZYZ, with its mixture of loud bass-orientated music and regional news. Bertram listened for a while, hoping that his exchange with the taxi driver had come to an end; then he turned all his attention to the island of his boyhood.

On the far side of the road there was little but sugar cane, which swam out flat like some vast economic blight. On the near side of the road the slack sea, the waves too sluggish to break. This one road hugged the perimeter of the island as though afraid to stray inland, and in the course of its thirty-mile circle it passed through a dozen irregularly spaced villages. Taking this particular route around the island meant that Sandy Bay, if Bertram remembered properly, would be the fifth village they would come to. Now, up ahead, he could see they were approaching the first. A few houses began to litter both sides of the road. Standing impassively outside them were small trouserless children with vests that just covered their distended bellies.

Most went barefoot, but a few wore a solitary shoe which reminded Bertram that as children they used to joke that a child with only one shoe had a dead mother. Now, as he thought of his own mother, he found it disturbing to remember that he had once been amused by such humourless games.

The houses in this first village were wooden shacks painted all colours, as though a rainbow had bent down and licked some life into the place. They were framed by green vegetation which to Bertram's eyes seemed almost plastic in its perfection. He watched as a mother furiously beat a piece of rope across the back of a child's legs, the child silent, his face twisted in concentration. And then the taxi moved on past the snarling dogs. Bertram rolled down the window and listened to the music from both radio and throat, spiritually rich music for it came from the heart where people cried when they were happy and laughed when they were sad. They passed the stove-weary mothers putting braids in their small daughters' hair with metal comb and oil for tool and lubrication, their husbands squatting on wooden boxes before a tray of dominoes. Bertram looked at the cane cutters who were now free for the day, but still walked like condemned men with neither hope nor desire, their arms swinging loosely by their sides, as if they had just witnessed the world turn a full circle knowing that fate no longer held any mystery for them. And he looked at the young girls waggling their hips crazily and throwing out their chests where breasts did not yet exist. Bertram found himself overwhelmed and disturbed by the bare brown legs, tired black limbs, rusty minds, the bright kinetic reds of the village signalling birth, the pale weary greens the approach of death. For a moment he could not admit to himself that he was home.

'People seem just as poor as they always been,' said Bertram.

The man looked back at him but said nothing, as though unsure whether his passenger spoke from embarrassment or disappointment. Bertram caught the driver's look, but quickly turned away.

Although taken aback by the poverty of this village, it was the general optimism of the populace that now began to occupy Bertram's attention. In the midst of this tropical squalor, people were conscientiously repairing properties and dressing them with decorations. Others were whitewashing walls and cutting down overhanging branches. The tree trunks were painted white so they looked like long black legs sporting freshly-laundered tennis socks. And the bunting was strung from branch to branch, from telegraph pole to telegraph pole, with the small flags of independence scattered everywhere. But it was impossible for Bertram to ignore the existence of a conflict between the optimism of this imminent independence, and the outward signs of a village still struggling to acquire the means to meet the most basic of needs, such as running water and proper lighting. He wondered if he was suffering from those same feelings of liberal guilt that he had always despised in some English people, or if in fact his thoughts did contain astute insights into the current state of the island.

As they moved into the heart of the next village, the taxi slowed down as the people grew thicker and claimed the outer fringes of the road as legitimate territory for their games and loitering. Then magically the people began to thin again, and the taxi was able to speed up and accelerate away into the country. The road was deserted, apart from the odd group of girls, their bodies slim as Coca-Cola bottles, making their way home from school in their regulation khaki uniforms. Following close behind them were the boys, their books balanced neatly on their heads to protect them from the sun. From the fields which skirted this section of the road curled great billowing clouds of smoke. The leaves were being burnt off the canestalks to make them easier to cut. The flames licked the air and the cindered canetrash spun in the wind. As they walked on the schoolchildren protected their eyes against the smoke. Then a bus crashed by, its engine aimlessly over-revved. Bertram watched as it bounced on its springs like an animated toy, stopping up the road ahead to set down a group of tired cutters. The old brakes hissed, cursed, then savoured the relief of a moment's peace. Having taken its rest the bus shuddered and belched before disappearing behind a greyish mist of spent fuel.

Sandy Bay was the only village on the island, apart from the capital, Baytown, which possessed another road besides Island Road. The road was called Whitehall, but a thoroughfare less like London's Whitehall would be hard to imagine. It forked off left from Island Road, and the taxi immediately reduced speed as it entered the narrow highway. The road had been made because it led down to the pier, a rickety construction erected by a previous administration. The pier jutted out into the sea in the hope that it might facilitate trade with, and thus appease, the natives on one of the two sister islands, an island so far away that its low outline could only be observed on the clearest of days. But this sister island had refused to be mollified, and eventually she had insisted upon her 'freedom' from what she considered to be a double colonial yoke. The British listened patiently to the islanders' pleadings, then decided that the most practical thing to do would be to invade the sister island. Six thousand paratroopers landed on an island barely six miles long, and people woke up that morning and found it raining Red Berets. The island's three policemen ran to the station and fought over the two rifles. And having restored order the British secured for this island its own sovereignty, and Whitehall became an even narrower road, and the pier at its end fell into disrepair.

'Stop by the ghaut,' said Bertram.

'By the Sutton house there?'

The taxi driver pointed to a large concrete house that was painted a blossomy orange. It was set so close to the road that the low wire fence surrounding it looked like an embroidered hem. To squeeze between it and the walls of the house would be difficult, if not impossible, so all the fence served to do was make sure that the walls of the house were not the edge of the road.

'I suppose so,' said Bertram. 'But I don't remember the house.'

'You wouldn't,' said the driver with the satisfaction of one-upmanship. 'It's only been there five or six years. But you remember the Suttons?'

'Sure,' said Bertram. Mr Sutton had been a teacher at

the Baytown Girls' High School, and his dominating wife had looked after the Sunday School classes in Sandy Bay. He wondered if they were still alive. If they were they would be old, but at least they had managed to save enough money over the years to have a concrete house, although something inside Bertram told him they were probably less comfortable in this house than they had been in their old wooden one. It seemed that the desire for symbols of affluence touched even the most pious of souls.

The taxi came to a halt, and the man screwed himself around in his seat and scratched the grey bristles on his craggy face.

'I think we agreed upon thirty dollars, isn't it?'

Bertram lifted his backside from the seat and slipped a hand into his pocket. He peeled off a purple note and two green ones, and passed the money to the man, who received it with silence.

'You're not going to help me with the cases?' asked Bertram.

The driver got out of the car and Bertram followed. Having removed the suitcases he turned to Bertram, who was now looking overhead. An aeroplane streaked across the sky leaking a thin wisp of smoke, its noise rising and dying like that of a wave. Bertram knew now that he was alone, as he watched the jet that had brought him home continue its journey south.

'You needing a hand down the ghaut with these?'

'As far as the gate would be useful.'

Bertram picked up the large suitcase and left the lighter one for the disabled man.

The ghaut was the ghaut of his childhood. A thin

dusty path that led down into what could almost be considered a separate village. It was flanked on either side by tightly-crammed, ill-balanced and blistered shacks that looked as though they might at any moment split open and reveal the bleakness inside. Underneath these houses played the children and fowls, while the sun-blackened adults tended to the sporadic yam or cassava plants that speckled the yard. Above them towered the stubborn breadfruit trees, pregnant with food, and together with the thick rubbery banana leaves, the wispier leaves of the palm, and the blazing red of the hibiscus, they created a spectacle of foliage through which only the sharpest spokes of light could penetrate. The air smelt of food being reheated in large blackened pots, and was stung with the faint echo of a vibrant drug. Running down the centre of the ghaut were thin metal pipelines which Bertram realized were new to him, and he had to take extra care not to trip over them. Then, about half-way down on the right, he saw the house in which he had been born, the house in which he had grown up with his mother and his younger brother. It had recently received a lick of paint, or, more correctly, many licks. Bertram felt both glad that the place was being looked after, and appalled that the medley of colours was so distasteful.

'This is it,' he said to the taxi driver as he put down his suitcase. The driver set down the other suitcase by the gate.

'You have everything?' he asked, clearly out of breath.

Bertram nodded. As he turned the man tugged at the waistline of his baggy pants, and Bertram watched him tack his way back up the ghaut towards his car.

Two small boys stood by the gate and looked up at Bertram. They both sported tee-shirts emblazoned with the new flag of independence. He looked at them and tried to imagine whose children they were, sure that their parents must once have been childhood friends, but he could not trace their origins. Then he looked down and noticed that they were standing with open palms. Although they asked for nothing, he realized they were begging and this annoyed him. Bertram picked up both suitcases.

The gate still hung drunkenly from its hinges. It creaked as he pushed it, and slammed loudly as the now-rusty spring flipped it back into place. The family house was little more than a two-roomed box built up on tiny pillars of bricks so that animals might find shade from the heat of the sun and shelter from the downpours during the rainy season. Four clearly unstable steps led to the front door, which in Bertram's memory had never been opened. Bertram could see the back of a chest of drawers which made the door impossible to open. The steps were for sitting on and talking to people who might lean over the fence.

Bertram left the two suitcases just inside the gate and made his way around to the back of the house. The kitchen stood in the middle of the dirt yard, the door open, the inside cluttered and untidy, reminding him of an English toolshed. A dog was licking out the contents of what Bertram imagined to be an empty pot of soup, so he bent and picked up a pebble. He tossed it and dashed the dog on the side of its head; then he watched as it scampered off, knocking over the pot as it did so. From inside the house no voice was raised to ask what was going on, no irate face appeared at the door, no item was thrown out to make doubly sure that the dog did not return. Bertram realized that either his mother was out, or she was sound asleep.

He climbed the steps that led to the back door, and brushed aside the curtain he remembered watching his mother hang when he was scarcely five years old. Then he stopped and looked around the cramped room. The same curling postcards and photographs, once coloured, now yellow and white, were tucked under the same ceiling beams, were pinned to the same walls with the same drawing pins, were propped up against the same hymn books and unopened novels. The room disturbed him for it looked like a museum, but a special kind of museum where only he could be aware of the significance of the items on exhibition.

From the next room he could hear an uncomfortable breathing, as though the person was inhaling sand. Bertram eased back a second curtain (hung, if he remembered rightly, at the same time as the first) and stared at his mother. She lay on her back, arms by her sides, rigid as though Bertram ought to file past her rather than stand and look. It was a particularly warm evening and her face was puffed and wet with perspiration. As the breeze rose and swung the single light bulb, its glow caught his mother's skin and she held its reflection as though it were the most precious treasure on earth. But Bertram could see her face was thinner, the cheeks higher and more pronounced. Her hair was now a dignified silvery-grey, and the high veins on her arms criss-crossed as though a wire netting just below the skin was holding her together. She seemed at home in her bed, and Bertram wondered if the rest of her small house held any interest for her. It was impossible for him to judge the state of her mind as he had not heard from her in many years. Their letters to each other, though never frequent, seemed to have dried up like a river bed in summer. Whatever it was that had flowed between them had suddenly ceased, and Bertram's greatest fear was that he might return home and find that his mother had died and nobody, not even Dominic, had bothered to write and let him know. Then his mother stirred, and instinctively Bertram stood back and tried to find some shadow. But she did not open her eyes. She simply relaxed back into the same spasmodic pattern of breathing, and Bertram took this opportunity to retreat into the front room. Once there he hovered by the small settee, wanting to fold it out and lie down, but he thought he should first bring in the suitcases from outside.

The two boys still stood by the gate holding out their hands as though some form of paralysis had set in. Bertram looked at the suitcases, then at the two boys, then up and down the ghaut to make sure that nobody was watching. He pushed his hand into his pocket and, unsure as to why he was doing so, he gave the two boys ten pence each. They looked at the round silver coins that now lay in the middle of their palms, unable to decide what to do with them. They did not recognize the coins but they looked valuable, big and heavy. Then, presumably having assumed that they had been given something of great worth, they both quickly smiled and ran off as fast as they could before the man changed his mind. Bertram watched them, the tops of their short legs barely thickening out into dusty buttocks, their tee-shirts still white, knowing full well that by the time independence arrived these government gifts would be little more than soiled rags.

Bertram turned and picked up the suitcases. Then he saw that the dog had reappeared and was sitting and looking at him, as though guarding the door to the kitchen. He glared back and considered throwing yet another pebble, but it dawned on him that the animal might belong to his mother, so he strode past it and up the steps and into the house. The absurdity of his luggage became clear, for the two suitcases took up most of the floor area. He had no idea where he would eventually find space to unpack, and was uncertain about what would follow when he had done so. Bertram pushed both suitcases to one side and slumped on to the solitary chair, sleep stealing into his body. The tension of the flight, and the subsequent heat of a Caribbean day was beginning to oppress him. He tried to slouch in the high-backed wooden chair that his mother called 'a preacherman chair', its plain structure giving off an unmistakable air of religious discomfort, but the small ball of fire at the base of his spine simply encouraged him to twist and turn until he finally resigned himself to this ordeal of pain. Bertram put his feet up on one of the suitcases, loosened the top button of his shirt, and slackened off his tie. Then he smiled inwardly as he realized that he had returned. There had been moments in the last twenty years when he felt sure he would never have the courage or the means to set foot once again on his island.

Bertram had left the island a wayward boy who had seized a final opportunity to fulfil his potential. Father Daniels, the English vicar, had seen to it that Bertram sat for the scholarship, even though nobody thought this restive boy could possibly succeed. A neighbour had told his mother that it was sinful to waste good ink and paper, but although she had never set any great store by academic achievement his mother was willing to defend either of her sons in anything they said they wanted to do.

On the morning of the scholarship examination his mother rose early to prepare for him a special breakfast, so he could at least start the day on an equal footing with the other boys. She fried some plantain and saltfish, then cut up a ten-cents loaf and made a sauce for him to dip his bread into. Dominic, his younger brother, ate his meal in silence. Then he began to rush, as though anxious to eat more than Bertram, but when his mother shouted at him he threw down his fork, snatched up his bag, and sprinted off towards school.

'Dominic, come back here, you hear me! You don't even comb your hair as yet!'

In their mother's eyes this was by far the greater of the crimes he had committed. Bertram tried not to look up for he felt his brother's behaviour was a deliberate ploy to upset him and make him lose concentration. So he continued to eat, and redoubled his efforts to think about the English, and the History, and the preliminary questions of Law that Father Daniels had been filling his head with for the last two years. Last year he had tried to convince Father Daniels that he was ready to take the examination, but Father Daniels had counter-argued that he liked to prepare a boy properly. Half-preparation was of no use to anyone. But in his heart Bertram had worried that by the time he was allowed to sit for the scholarship, he would be so old that people would laugh at him. And true enough when it was announced he would be doing so, some had laughed at him. At nineteen he was made to feel ancient, even though most of the others were nearly his age, two or three years out of school with some benevolent adult instructing them, either an old teacher or a friend of the family. And now, on this critical day, the twelve candidates were finely tuned and prepared, and expected to perform like racehorses.

Bertram found a desk at the back of the furthest column of six, across the aisle from his friend. Jackson Clayton was of stout medium build and the proud possessor of elegant good looks. Bertram had a gawkishly juvenile body, his neck like a slender stalk that held too weighty a flower. Jackson's features, in addition to his being the captain of the youth cricket team, meant he had little problem in attracting the girls. Why he was sitting the examination was a mystery to many, though of course most expected him to take the scholarship, he being somebody who seemed destined to succeed at anything he put his hand or mind to.

On one of those long evenings down by the abandoned pier, when Bertram would bowl to Jackson over after over of soft ball spin, so that his friend could practise dropping a dead bat on it and killing the kick on the ball, Jackson had admitted to Bertram that his father had threatened to beat him if he did not make an effort for the scholarship. Jackson claimed that he had protested forcibly, even though he knew full well he would finally lose out to the wishes of his father. And so, like Bertram, he had ended up taking tuition from Father Daniels, even though his greatest wish was to remain on the island and some day open the batting for the West Indies. It was a big ambition, in fact the biggest. Bertram had continued to bowl to him until the night began to mop up the blood from the sun, and in the distance the moon appeared, as yet unseen. He thought Jackson might some day make the team, but Bertram knew Jackson would never win the scholarship. It was pride alone that had made him enter. The idea of being thought ignorant had been a greater spur than any threat of parental beatings, but Bertram said nothing for he never argued with his friend. He continued to bowl to him until the brooding trees waved their spreading heads in time with the rhythms of the sea breeze, and eventually it was too dark to continue.

Father Daniels was to be their invigilator. He stood at the front of the schoolroom and took a small paper knife to the brown package, which they all assumed contained their papers. Jackson rearranged his ruler and pencil, one behind the other, then turned to his friend.

'You feeling nervous, man?'

Bertram nodded. 'I feel like all the knowledge is just draining out of my head.'

'You lucky then, for I didn't never have none in my head to start with.'

They both looked up at Father Daniels, his balding head catching the sun as he bent almost double and tried now to break manually into the envelope. He was a dignified man, unimposing in stature and modest of voice, a perfect combination for teaching boys in their late adolescence.

'You didn't listen to what Father Daniels been telling you?' asked Bertram.

''Course I listened,' said Jackson, 'but I don't want to go to England. I have a job in the bank, and I have the bat, man. Anyhow, I hope you win for when you gone I going check for Patsy Archibald.'

'How you know if I win I won't take she with me?'

'Don't chat shit, man. The scholarship fund don't provide for women.'

'So what happen if the victor have a wife?'

Jackson picked up his pencil and pointed it at Bertram.

'You making joke with me, Bertram? You can't be serious about marriage to a girl like that.'

'Like what?' snapped Bertram, indignation rising inside of him. 'Like what?' he demanded.

Having finally wrestled open the packet, Father Daniels now looked up at them both. His ruddy face was calm and he spoke quietly, a whisper that only just managed to reach the back of the room.

'Francis and Clayton, are you two boys interested in the scholarship paper or would you rather go outside and continue your discussion there?' He stared at them both, but neither said anything. 'Well?'

'Sorry, Father Daniels,' they chorused simultaneously.

Father Daniels looked hard at them; then having reasserted his authority he pulled the papers from the envelope and began to distribute them. Bertram sneaked a look at Jackson, who grinned. They had both failed their first unscheduled test, and nobody would expect either of them now to pass the examination. The other ten boys sat in front, seemingly calm outside, but Bertram felt sure that inside they too were racked with nerves.

When Father Daniels reached Bertram he let his hand linger on the desk. He seemed loath to let go of the examination paper and, fed up with looking at his hand, it occurred to Bertram that perhaps Father Daniels wanted him to look up. When he did so Bertram read a private message. Father Daniels was clearly annoyed with him for what had just taken place, but he was also delivering a short final tutorial in which no words were necessary. His steely glare said everything. As Father Daniels made his way back towards the front of the class, Jackson turned to Bertram and inquisitively raised his eyebrows, but Bertram simply let a fraternal smile crease his face.

'You boys have three hours in which to complete the paper as best you can. I don't want to hear any talking or conferring. I don't want to see anybody looking at anybody else's paper, and I wish you all the best of luck. God's will shall prevail, and may the best young man succeed.'

Bertram picked up his paper then froze, suddenly afraid to take a look and see what the three questions were that he would have to answer. He turned to his right and stared through the open door. Out at sea a pair of boats were making their way back to the island after a night of fishing. They were late, thought Bertram. Usually the boats had landed and the fish been sold by now, and without warning Bertram found his mind totally occupied with the various reasons that might explain their overdue arrival. A shark, an illness, a broken rudder, an extra large catch that had handicapped them? The options were almost endless, and for a few moments they proved more interesting than the paper in front of him. Above the boat he saw a giant bird carefully riding an air current. Then it dropped in a long and barely perceptible curve, and without a ripple it emerged with a large silver fish twice its size.

The papers were sent to England for marking, and it was two months before the boys were due to meet again in the schoolroom. In this time Jackson achieved the great honour of being selected to attend the West Indies youth team camp on a neighbouring island. He was also invited to the Governor's house, and Jackson told Bertram that he had shaken hands not only with the Governor, but with the Governor's wife. He also claimed to have patted the white horse that the Governor kept around the back of the house, but Bertram knew there was no white horse. While Jackson's fame reached new heights, Bertram found himself grappling with the multiple problems of work, his brother, and most crucially, Patsy Archibald. Suddenly, as though being punished, Bertram's life became unbearably complicated.

He had found himself in a trough of depression after the scholarship examination, and so he left his job with the municipal department. This loss had troubled him little, as he had been not much more than a glorified litter collector in Stanley Park. And although his new job stacking shelves at Vijay's Supermarket was hardly much of an improvement, it did mean he had a few extra dollars in his pocket and some privacy in his work. At the end of the day he now began to hang around in Baytown, for he could afford to buy a beer, and stand up laughing in the street with the other young men, then go around the back of the treasury building and piss his spent water in a loud and lordly arch. But his leisurely behaviour, although largely ignored by his mother, was something that began to drive a wedge between himself and Dominic.

Because of their father's perpetual absence, Dominic had come to depend upon Bertram more than a younger brother would normally do. They played together, ate together, slept and worked, they even lost their virginity together, having persuaded a local girl that if she did it twice it would be impossible for her to get pregnant. Bertram had gone first, then watched as Dominic conjured a stiffness into himself and entered. Bertram trusted his younger brother enough to tell him that this was his first time, although in the past he had lied to him, sure that Dominic needed to hear stories of fictional conquest in order to reinforce the notion of his older brother as a special being. But now that Bertram seemed to be spending more time in town after work, Dominic was becoming increasingly isolated. These days when he returned home from town, Bertram would often find his younger brother asleep, and in the morning loath to talk to him.

When Bertram started to see Patsy Archibald, Dominic became even more distant. They had both known Patsy for years, and although she was Bertram's age she was Dominic's friend too, for that was the way that it had always been. Like them, she was being brought up by just the one adult, although in her case it was not her mother but her aunt, for both parents had emigrated to Canada. One day, as they lay by the sea on the thin black scrap of sand that was a beach for the people of Sandy Bay, Bertram became aware of her in a manner which frightened him. He let her hand paddle in his palm, and the heat from her body aroused him. Then, having conquered his initial fear, he smiled at her and felt his body invaded with sexual longing. Suddenly the sole purpose of their afternoon involved divorcing themselves from Dominic. He was too adult for either of them to suggest he went to the shop or for a walk so, as the sun drew the strength from them like a giant sponge, they simply waited.

An hour later Dominic peeled himself off the sand and stood up. He was tall, and it was possible he might one day outgrow his brother. But Dominic was a nascent oak as opposed to a willowy sapling. He looked at the pair of them, lying flat on their backs and squinting up at the sky, then he brushed the sand from his legs and arms.

'It's too hot for me,' he announced.

Bertram propped himself up on one elbow and tried to look as though he was in some way distressed by his brother's imminent departure.

'So where you going that don't be hot?'

'I don't know,' said Dominic. 'Probably back home to sit inside. I don't know how the two of you don't start to steam then cook.'

Like Bertram, Patsy now propped herself up on her elbow. She continued to squint as she looked at Dominic.

'I know what you mean,' she said. 'But I going maybe lie here just a short while longer.'

'Well, I can't take it no more,' said Dominic.

He turned and left them. They both watched as he walked along the beach, then up the back of a small dune and out of sight. Patsy looked across at Bertram, and although he felt her eyes he could not meet them. Then he heard Patsy lower herself down on to the sand.

'You want to go now?' asked Bertram, his eyes firmly fixed upon the sea.

Patsy said nothing. Up above them a gull made a noise like an airborne cat. Then Bertram felt pressured by her silence into looking at her. When he did so he was sure that she had deliberately forced this quiet upon him so that he would have to make the first overtly suggestive move.

'So why you don't kiss me, Bertram?'

Bertram looked at her small and ideally-formed body, and his eyes caressed her high breasts. But he was still unsure of what was happening between them.

'Well?' said Patsy. 'I know both you and Dominic had girls before, but it's you I want.'

Bertram felt confused. 'You ever take a man?' he asked.

Patsy laughed and sat up straight. She looked into Bertram's eyes as though shocked by his diffidence.

'Bertram, you honestly think that if I'd have had a next man I'd be waiting for you to touch me? Bertram, please do something or I going take fright and leave this place.'

Bertram leaned forward and kissed her roughly, not because he felt a lack of sensitivity towards her, but because he was off-balance. Then he ran his hand clumsily along her leg, as though trying to wipe something off it, but Patsy trapped his hand with hers. She began to strip off his shirt, and as Bertram opened his mouth to speak she kissed silence into his body. Steering him towards her she encouraged him to stiffen, taut like a bow, then slowly she helped him to break into a thick milky predicament. She eased Bertram over to one side and lay back happy and at peace. But Bertram was restless, his mind turning over, his feet itching for he could feel the sand that had squeezed its way between shoe and sock.

When he returned home Dominic was sitting on the front steps that led nowhere, fanning himself with a coconut palm leaf. Bertram stopped at the gate. At first he simply looked as a neighbour's black pigs scampered to and fro, their snouts twitching, their eyes as ever wet. Then he could no longer tolerate the tension.

'You cool enough now?' asked Bertram.

Dominic glanced up at him. Then he looked back down at the space between his own feet.

'What's the matter, little man?' Bertram pushed open the gate. 'Something the matter with Mummy?' Dominic neither spoke nor looked up. 'You lost your tongue?'

'You fuck Patsy?' asked Dominic. 'You wait till I gone to fuck her?'

Bertram sighed.

'I fucked her, but I didn't wait until you gone to do it. Or rather I did, but it's not something I planned.'

Dominic was looking up at him now, his face contorted in hurt, and Bertram knew that whatever he said he was bound to make it more painful for his brother. However, before he could say any more Dominic got to his feet and ran from him around the back of the house and slammed the door. He leaned against the gate and heard his mother angrily telling Dominic not to make so much noise. Bertram knew if he were to go in his presence would only serve to trigger off his brother's fury once again, but as he looked around he knew he could not stand by the gate all night. So he chose instead to go for a walk, and soon he found himself outside the schoolroom.

Bertram walked around the front of the building and tried the door. It opened, and he resolved to go in and sit down until he felt secure enough that it would be all right to go back and confront both Dominic and his mother. But when he woke up it was morning, and the hand on his shoulder was that of Father Daniels, the same Father Daniels who stood before him on the morning that was to change his life.

Father Daniels looked at all twelve boys. He knew that to them two months must seem like a long time, but he found it difficult to believe that things had been decided so quickly, and that the critical letter had already arrived from England. He fingered the piece of paper and checked himself, realizing that he was playing with them for there was only the one name to read out, and he could hold that name quite comfortably in his head.

'The winner of this year's island scholarship is Bertram Francis of Sandy Bay.'

All eyes turned upon Bertram. Most were disbelieving, but some looked momentarily relieved, even pleased that it was not them. After all, Bertram knew that not every boy had wanted to sit the examination, parental ambition often being a cruel spur to childhood labour.

'He will be going to England', continued Father Daniels, 'to pursue his chosen topic of study which, as I'm sure you're all aware, will be in the Law.'

Father Daniels betrayed no emotion as he stared directly at Bertram.

'Well, I think you might all give your colleague a round of applause. His is an achievement worthy of your appreciation.'

As they did so Bertram was filled with an inner conflict, unsure whether or not he should stand up to receive their congratulations. But mercifully their applause soon died away, and he was no longer required to make a decision.

Dominic was still at school when Bertram returned home with the good news. He picked his way down the ghaut and saw his angular mother carrying water from the standpipe to the kitchen. She wore a green headscarf which only seemed to accentuate the long rake of her face, and deepen the hollow blackness where her eyes should have been. There could be little doubt as to whose features Bertram had inherited. She looked up at him and spoke without breaking step.

'You not working today, then?'

Bertram felt certain that he had told her this was the day the results came through, but he could not be sure. Rather than imagine that his mother might have forgotten, he preferred to look upon himself as the one who had suffered an aberration of memory.

'I had to go up by the schoolroom to see Father Daniels.'

'And what it is he have to say for himself?'

'He say I win the scholarship from the island to go to England.'

His mother stopped and stared at him. For what seemed an age they said nothing to each other, then she spoke, although by now the focus of her eyes had slackened and Bertram could no longer be sure that she was looking at him.

'I'm proud of you, Bertram.'

As though unable to think of anything else to say she turned and walked away, and Bertram felt sure that she did not understand the full implications of his achievement.

Bertram sat on the fence and looked up the ghaut. The line of his body fell from his narrow shoulders to his feet, with no discernible deviation either inward or outward. When he perched on the fence he did so as a bird, tucking one leg up under the other, flamingo-style. He would not bother going in to work today for there was too much to think about. Then he looked over into the next yard where a young boy tried to fly a kite which leapt feebly on the thin breeze before once more plummeting back to the ground. He watched for a while, then realized it would be hours before Dominic returned. He jumped down and decided to take a stroll. As Bertram passed up the ghaut he saw the market-women sitting in their well-broomed backyards, their breasts like blackening mushrooms, shrivelled, waterless and undesirable. They were crouched, feet shrouded in outsize laceless shoes, flicking at the insects, aprons filthy, pockets bulging with useless change, and their broad straw hats only made complete by the occasional gaping hole. They had already been to Baytown and sold what bits of fruit and vegetable they had managed to gather or scrape up from the land, and now their day was done. Behind them, and stacked in discarded piles, lay rusting junk, and huddled beside the lumber their elevated shacks had their doors and windows thrown wide open trying to catch what little wind there was. The extremes of heat and rain, the habitual lashing from a hurricane or a movement of the earth, meant that these crooked dwellings seldom lasted long, but they did cast large pools of shadow in which animals were able to sleep.

Bertram looked at the marketwomen but kept walking until he reached Whitehall. Once there he glanced across the road and up and through the length of the village. But the shop doorways, the concrete steps, the grass verges, were strewn with sun-stunned villagers standing, sitting, drinking, ignoring the flies and the heat and dust, staring at nothing. It was the dull season around Sandy Bay so there was no longer cane to cut. Bertram decided to go back home and sit up on the fence. He was too familiar with the misery of the scenes that filled his eyes, and today of all days he wanted to think beyond them.

He sat again on the fence and tried hard to imagine what England would be like. He thought of how disciplined he would have to be in his study if he was to live up to what was now expected of him, not only by Father Daniels but by everyone on the island. These thoughts flashed backward and forward through the troubled cinema of his mind and before he knew it, time had slipped by and the sky began to darken.

When he finally saw Dominic the day was at an end. He was carrying a cricket bat so Bertram knew exactly what he had been doing. Dominic walked slowly, clearly exhausted at this late hour by what Bertram imagined to have been a keenly fought contest. He waited until his brother was right below him before speaking.

'You win the game?' began Bertram.

'We didn't play no match.'

Dominic leaned the bat off against the fence, as though aware that they would probably be talking with each other for quite some while.

'We just play until the man is out and a next one to go in.'

'I see,' said Bertram, nodding aimlessly. 'You bat?'

'Most of the night,' said his brother, trying not to show any pride in his achievement. There was a chance, slim though it was, that Dominic might one day mature into a decent batsman. However, unlike Bertram's friend Jackson, it was not a goal he was actively pursuing to the exclusion of all others.

'Well, I have a piece of news I want to tell you before I tell anyone else.'

Dominic looked over his brother's shoulder, enquiring as to whether or not Bertram had already told their mother his news. Bertram knew he would have to respond to this unasked question.

'I had to tell her first for you weren't here.'

Dominic gave him an empty look which left Bertram unsure if his brother was interested in what he was trying to say to him. Then Dominic spoke.

'You capture the scholarship, right?'

Bertram nodded. 'Who tell you?'

'Twelve of you sitting in the room when Father Daniels announce the winner. You think the other eleven going keep their mouth shut?'

Bertram was piqued that Dominic should speak to him in this way, but he was also secretly pleased that his brother should, for what he considered to be the first time, have outsmarted him.

'I see what you mean,' said Bertram, in as generous a voice as he could muster.

Dominic picked up his bat and pushed open the crooked gate. He passed through into the yard and let the gate swing shut behind him.

'You don't have nothing to say to me, then? No congratulations or anything of that order?'

Bertram realized he was letting Dominic know how upset he was, but he could not control himself. Dominic looked down and began to strike at the dust with the blade of his bat.

'This mean you're going to England?' asked Dominic.

'Of course it means I'm going to England,' said Bertram. He leapt off the fence and circled around to face his brother.

'People don't take the scholarship examination to pass it and stay here. I'm going to England, but only for three years, four years at the most.'

Dominic lifted his head, and his eyes met those of his older brother. Bertram knew that what had happened between himself and Patsy had soured their relationship, but this new blow was something that Dominic had clearly feared and half-anticipated for much longer. He looked hard at his younger brother, but it was as though Dominic could not find it within his heart to be angry at him. Bertram watched as Dominic let the bat slide through his hand, then with a quick flick of his wrist the wandering bat was back in his grip.

Dominic turned and walked off towards the house. Bertram's eyes followed him, still trying to understand his brother's distress, but he thought it best to leave him on his own for a few moments. Rather than leap back up on the fence, Bertram decided to take a walk up the ghaut and buy a beer at Mr Carter's shop.

There was no street lighting in Sandy Bay, let alone ghaut lighting. Bertram edged his way up the ghaut, but he found it impossible to make this journey without treading on something uneven, although it was usually little more than a piece of broken cane lying chewed and rejected like a limb snapped in half. At the top of the ghaut some boys were sitting on the side of the road, soaking up whatever heat still lay unspent from the day. They waved to Bertram, more a gesture of new respect than a greeting or sign of imminent departure.

Leslie Carter's shop stood alone, its wooden walls thin with age, its roof inadequate. Outside, someone had nailed up a mosaic of bright enamel signs that advertised foreign beer, aspirins, and Pepsi-Cola. Inside, and carelessly displayed on the shelves, were the familiar packages of skin cream, soap powder, hair shampoo, all of them with healthy pink faces on the packets. On top of the counter Mr Carter kept some cold meat, though it was regularly peppered with flies as he usually forgot to cover it over once he had cut off a piece. And beside the meat was a large glass case in which there were cakes and stale patties.

The proprietor was folded over the shop counter. He wore his familiar orange vest and sported a tidemarked hat, the sort of hat a cowboy would wear, wide in the brim, tall in the crown. Bertram climbed the couple of steps and settled himself on one of the homemade stools. The ritual began. Mr Carter knew exactly what Bertram wanted, but he would not be rushed into getting it until he was ready. He looked at Bertram and waited, as though listening to some night symphony heard solely by himself and his dog. Only when the last strains of this 'music' had died away did he unfold himself and turn around. He lifted the lid of the freezer and took out a bottle of beer that was thinly frosted with ice. He slotted it into the wall-opener, as if ready to break off the neck of the bottle, and watched with infantile fascination as the metal cap fell obediently into the tin tray placed there for that purpose.

'Fifty cents.'

Bertram pushed a dollar across the counter, and Mr Carter picked it up as though this might be his last ever act. Tiredness flooded his every move, and to a stranger it might appear as though he were suffering from a debilitating disease that was eating away at either the muscles of his body or the fabric of his mind. But Bertram, like everyone else in the village, understood that this was just the way he was. There was no simpler or more complex explanation of his behaviour than that. Mr Carter had nothing to hurry for, he never had, and he never would. He slapped down Bertram's change, then he turned and once more folded himself over the counter. Bertram looked at him and realized that tonight there would be no conversation, for the second movement of Mr Carter's night symphony had already commenced. He picked up the bottle and took a drink. The beer was so cold it tasted metallic and he gasped. Then he screwed himself around so he too could look out over the side street of Whitehall. The alternative was to continue staring at the cans of bully beef, and the soup, and the brown bags of sugar, and the countless packs of batteries that were piled up behind the food in anticipation of the cricket season. If there was one thing you could always rely upon Mr Carter to have, it was batteries. To run out when a cricket match was coming up would lose him more custom than any amount of bad manners could possibly do.

When Bertram reached home the lights were off. He knew his mother would be asleep by now, but he was convinced that Dominic would still be awake. Bertram undressed in the yard. He stripped off down to his underpants, then carrying his clothes under one arm he curled himself around the door, through the curtain, and into the house. He could see Dominic lying bulky in their bed, his back turned towards him. And in the next room he could hear his mother breathing with the cracked discord that often kept him awake, especially on hot nights such as this one.

'You awake, Dominic?'

He tried to whisper, not wanting to further annoy his brother. But although Dominic did not reply, Bertram felt sure that he was awake and simply playing games with him. He waited a moment and listened as a rat thumped about under the house, then he slid into bed and asked him again.

'Dominic, you awake?'

This time Bertram spoke with more urgency there was no reply, then Dominic stirred.

'Yes, I'm awake,' he said.

'I didn't wake you, did I?' asked Bertram.

'I'm awake,' said Dominic, in that same flat tone.

Bertram propped himself up and spoke once more.

'Look, you seem mad with me about winning the scholarship. You should be proud of me, man. I work hard for it, I thought you would be proud of me.'

There was a long silence before Dominic replied. When he did so he spoke softly.

'I am proud of you,' he said. 'But I can't believe you really care what I'm thinking any more. It's like I'm just a something you knew once and you suddenly coming on like you're big now.'

Although Bertram could not see his brother's face, he could feel the resentment in his voice.

'Dominic, you and me can't go on for the rest of our lives doing everything together.'

'We used to.'

'I know, but then things changed. I had to go to work, and I had to start to study for the scholarship and things.' He paused. 'Dominic, not everything can just carry on how it was, you know. Things always moving on but that don't mean we should fall out over them. We must learn to move in our own way too.'

'I don't want to change.'

'But that's just crazy, man!'

'You think you know everything now, don't you?!'

Dominic spun around to face him, his eyes rounded as though in fear.

'But you don't, you know. You're out with your new

friends like I don't exist or nothing, but you're wrong. You're so wrong that you're going to regret treating me like this. Like I'm still a boy and I can't do nothing with you!'

Bertram watched as Dominic's mouth expelled the words his heart had kept locked up for so long. And as he watched he saw a cloud burst inside his brother's head and a tear begin to trickle from the greyness of his eyes. He reached out a hand to touch him, but Dominic recoiled as though Bertram's body was charged with an electricity that might damage him were he to come into contact with it.

'What's the matter?' asked Bertram.

Dominic stared back as though he hated his older brother. Then he snatched up the cover around his neck and twisted away from him. All Bertram could now see was Dominic's back, which he could not keep still enough to hide the fact that he was sobbing into the sheet he held so closely to himself.

And now Bertram sat in the same room, his feet on a suitcase, and he listened to his mother's voice which only just managed to rise high enough to be supported by the still and humid air.

'Who it is through there? Mrs Sutton, it's you through there?'

Bertram reached up and loosened off his tie even further. His hands were itchy with dried sweat, and as he mopped his brow he realized he was caught in the fur-soft grip of a Caribbean night which had fallen quickly, as though in response to some unheard instruction. Outside he could see the clouds filtering the moon, and the shadows stood high like guards. Bertram listened to the chorus of insects, which he received as a constant roar. It disturbed him that he should have forgotten the pitch and echo of their massed voices, but it also reminded him of just how far he had travelled both in miles and time. He waited for a moment, unsure if his mother was going to call again; then he decided that his evasiveness might be frightening her.

His mother stared at him across the dimly lit room. Above her the swaying light bulb creamed everything in a pale yellow light. It hung from its beam, the wire twisted loosely around the wooden support as though a noose into which someone would soon slip their neck. His mother looked weary, her eyes glazed over with the age that had overtaken her during Bertram's absence.

'Hello, Mummy.'

Bertram walked slowly towards her. He leaned over and kissed her on the forehead, but she did not respond. Then he perched, uninvited, on the side of her bed and took her thin hands in his, but still she stared back at him as though he was not really there.

'See, I told you I'd come back.'

He laughed slightly, but his mother just looked at him. Then she dropped her eyes and began to roll her hands in the envelope of his, as though trying to make sure that her son was not simply a figment of her worn imagination.

'So you really done come back?'

'I've come back,' said Bertram, this time trying to make it less of an announcement.

'And when you planning on taking off again?'

Bertram knew that his mother's apparently casual enquiry was framed so as to lure him into a false sense of security. He cleared his throat before answering.

'I don't know if I'm planning on taking off anywhere again. I was thinking that I might stay here and try and find a position in the society and make back my peace with the island.'

He looked at his mother, but her gaze remained expressionless. Bertram felt obliged to continue, but he now found himself speaking to her as though trying to anticipate what she might be thinking.

'I know that twenty years is a long time to be away, but I feel that the time is right and I must seize the opportunity to help the new nation.'

'Help them how? It's only the school certificate that you left here with that you bringing back, am I wrong?'

'No, you're not wrong, but I have some money. I've managed to save a little, which should enable me to start up a business of some kind.'

'What kind of a business?'

It was only now that it became clear to Bertram his mother was speaking to him with an open contempt. And he discovered himself answering her with the polite manners of a schoolboy, as opposed to the self-assurance of a thirty-nine-year-old man.

'I don't know as yet what kind of a business, but something that don't make me dependent upon the white man.'

His mother began to smile. And then she laughed, at first with confidence, then with more control as though unsure if the fragility of her body could support too much humour.

'So that's what England teach you? That you must come home with some pounds and set up a business separate from the white man?'

Bertram looked at her as sternly as he dared. He spoke now with an indignation fuelled by his knowledge that she had seldom, in her sixty years on this earth, left Sandy Bay, let alone the island. To him her laughter was simply the cackle of ignorance, and he felt obliged to educate her.

'The only way the black man is going to progress in the world is to set up his own shops and his own businesses independent of the white man. There is no way forward for us if we keep relying on him, for we going continually be cleaning up his shit, and washing out his outhouse.'

'I see,' said his mother. 'And what white man has Leslie Carter ever worked for? If you take a walk up the ghaut in your smart English suit and tie, you going see him bent double like a tree in a high wind over the same counter you left him behind. Is that what you mean by progress?'

Bertram scrutinized his mother, but he could see that she had already switched off from him. He waited in the hope that she might revive their conversation, but eventually he decided to stand up from the bed and leave her to sleep. However, Bertram had to ask his mother just one more thing.

'How is Dominic?' he asked. 'He working still at the sugar factory?'

His mother's sigh was polluted with a high asthmatic whistle. Then she repeated Bertram's question.

'How is Dominic?'

After a few moments Bertram decided to speak out again.

'Well, Mummy. How is he?'

But Bertram could now see that his mother had fallen into a silence that made him wonder if she was sleeping. As he turned to take his leave her voice startled him.

'Your brother is well and waiting by the gate. We both going see him soon enough.'

Bertram turned back. He watched as his mother folded in her lips so they all but disappeared. As she did so her wretchedness became evident.

In the morning Bertram found himself fully clothed and curled up foetus-style in the chair. Outside he could hear some children playing with a radio, spinning the dial from left to right, right to left, unable to decide upon any one station. He assumed that for them there would be no school today, and as the sun shot a dust-laden shaft through the window Bertram turned and thought of Dominic. He felt ashamed at having slept so soundly, but he knew that both nervous and physical exhaustion had finally taken their toll. Now he wanted to ask his mother more. He wanted to know how and when his brother had died, where he had died, and why he had not been told. But as he first looked at, then smelt the circles of sweat under his armpits, he knew he would have to wash and change before he could do anything else.

Bertram tried to spring from the chair, but he felt his back protest. He would have to be less adventurous. He leaned forward, opened one of the suitcases and from it he pulled a shirt. As he stood up he caught a mercifully quick glimpse of himself in the badly-silvered mirror that was propped up on the small table. His face was shaped like an isosceles triangle, the most acute apex being his stubbled chin, his eyes set high in the remaining two angles. He scratched some sleep from the corner of one eye, decided not to shave, then admitted to himself that the idea of going around the side of the house and washing under the standpipe, as he had done as a youngster, no longer appealed to him. At the moment he was prepared to remain a little grubby, so he got dressed.

He plucked aside the curtain and peered into his mother's room, where she was still anchored to her dreams. Bertram wanted to wake her, but fear overcame him. In the end he retreated into the front room and searched around in the trouser pockets of his suit for a few Eastern Caribbean dollars. Then he quietly made his way down the back steps and out into the bright morning. The first thing he noticed was the dog lying by the door to the kitchen. He was sure now that it must belong to his mother, for the dog looked up at him as if he were a trespasser on its property. Then Bertram saw the two boys to whom he had given the ten-pence pieces. They stood by the fence and stared at him. As he left the yard and turned to walk up the ghaut, their eyes silently followed him. 'They must know,' thought Bertram, as a bolt of guilt passed through him. He felt uneasy, and wished that they had become angry or accused him of deception or something. But as it was, he could only worry about his future meetings with the boys.

At the top of the ghaut Bertram turned right into Whitehall. Mr Carter was leaning over his counter, though characteristically he said nothing. Bertram smiled in his direction but it made little difference. He continued to walk up Whitehall, and although one or two people nodded at him the rest simply looked on, unsure as to whether this really was the Bertram Francis they thought it was. They squatted by the roadside, their eyes blurred and their feet swollen, watching their children drawing pictures in the dirt with pointed wooden sticks. And the children, they too looked at him. This puzzled Bertram until it occurred to him that in all probability they recognized a family likeness with Dominic. It was then that Bertram noticed some of the younger children seemed positively frightened, so he walked on at a quicker pace and listened as the villagers whispered to each other with dust-encrusted words.

The bus stop was where it had always been, outside the Browns' house and right across the road from the hospital. Though in reality there was no bus stop, just a place at the side of the road where horses and carriages had stopped long before the advent of the engine. Bertram looked across at the hospital and saw some workmen putting the final touches to an extension. A sign on the wall boasted that Princess Margaret, the Queen's representative, would be opening the 'new' hospital as part of this week's independence celebrations. The workmen scurried back and forth, hurrying to finish their work, but both to the left and to the right Bertram could see that little else in Sandy Bay had changed. The same houses were there, and Bertram imagined that the same people were doing the same things inside them. Only the festive streamers and slogans, and the images of the new flag painted up on the stone walls were unfamiliar. But when the bus arrived, Bertram noticed that at least one other aspect of life in Sandy Bay was new to his eyes, for this bus was clean and modern and trimmed with well-shined chrome. Bertram also noticed that it was not really a bus at all, but a refurbished Transit van with slick upholstery and a thumping hi-fi system. He climbed aboard and secured a seat by the offside window so he could look out to sea.

The bus was crowded with children taking advantage of their day off from school. Bertram looked at them and realized they were probably from St Patrick's. Due in part to its isolated position at the end of the island, this village had the reputation of harbouring the most backward of all the island's people. As a child Bertram had taken part in the many jokes about St Patrick's, but although he now recognized their triviality, he suspected that some people still made them. As he looked at the children and thought of St Patrick's, the bus sped away and began its frenzied journey to town. Bertram immediately remembered the style of driving, a style which seemed to be denying the possibility that there might be a tomorrow, and at the same time asserting the fact that the driver was a 'go-ahead' type of fellar. Each stop was sudden and threw passengers forward and careering into each other, each abrupt piece of acceleration designed to toss you from side to side and to impress upon you the fact that on this island speed was not measured by the speedometer, but by the number of bumps and bruises to the body.

As they raced towards Baytown, Bertram noticed that all the villages now seemed similar. There was generally a stop at the near end of the village, and one at the far end. Only at Middle Way was there also a stop in the centre, for this village was slightly larger than the others en route, though nowhere near the size of Sandy Bay. A little way out of Middle Way they lurched over two small humpbacked bridges, which to the untutored eye might appear to have no meaning. But unlike most dwarfish countries, where the river is a sinewy muscle, the strength of the place, rivers on this island were almost permanently sunk beneath their sun-baked bellies. Yet in times of rain they suddenly flowed as a torrent of water from the mountains cascaded down the hillsides, and if it were not for these bridges the island's highway would be severed in two places.

Once they had passed through Butler's village, the bus was able to accelerate down the long straight piece of road and into the gentle bend that gave them a view of Baytown, which from this distance looked beautiful. Behind the capital, and on the horizon, the sole surviving sister island brooded, clouds hanging over her as though harnessed to the mountain peaks by thin invisible wires. When Bertram thought of Baytown he pictured a tropical ghost town, like those they used to study in the geography lesson of the movies. He would queue for hours with his schoolfriends to watch the latest black and white westerns, the same movies they took their school nicknames from. Roy Rogers, Gary Cooper, Audie Murphy; Bertram had liked James Stewart best of all. His funny way of talking made Bertram feel sorry for him, but it also made him guess that to 'play' James Stewart would ensure his always being the object of some attention from his friends. But Cripple-mouth was what they decided to call him, until Bertram swore blind that he hated James Stewart and would never see another of his films.

In reality Baytown bore little resemblance to a mid-Western watering-hole. Father Daniels had taught Bertram that like most Caribbean towns, it was originally part slave-market and part harbour. It was primarily designed to facilitate the importation of Africans and the exportation of sugar, but over the years it had developed in three directions. Firstly, there were the well-patrolled middle-class estates of the possessors; neat, planned, perfumed, and often affording spectacular views of both the mountains and the sea. And then down by the harbour, and for a few streets in each direction, the low commercial buildings of trade and government. Finally, there existed a hellish and labyrinth-like entanglement of slums in which lived the dispossessed in their broken-down wooden buildings and under their rusty iron roofs. These dwellings were strung out like pebbles on a beach. They formed loosely-defined streets, some only wide enough to permit two cyclists to pass, and living self-consciously among them was always the odd concrete building whose slate roof sat a little easier on top. Streets that followed each other at random, streets in which awkward boys played cricket with no discipline, in which bad-tempered mongrels scoured every corner, crevice, crack for a morsel, in which hens played in drying and dried mud, and goats either wandered free or were tethered on chains so tight that one might as well have driven a bolt through the animals' heads into the thirsty earth. This area, which resembled the country in its poverty, had always impressed Bertram as the unassembled, peopled, animaled heart of Baytown.

Bertram stepped down from the bus and into the bright sunshine. The sound of the greasy fleckmarked sea filled his ears, and here in front of the treasury building, beside the pier that protruded like a finger pointing nowhere, the regular swell gave up pieces of driftwood and seaweed and other flotsam that spoiled the otherwise pleasant view. Along the bayfront Bertram saw people erecting their booths, small wooden structures painted all different colours, a busy population of garish blues and pinks. He knew it would not be long before the full festive atmosphere broke out in this temporary shanty town which, as the huge sign on the wall of Barclays Bank told him, would be known as Independence-ville. These booths specialized in selling all kinds of drink from rum to beer, from whisky to Coke, and a little food, curry or chicken, usually purchased and eaten as a stomach-liner in order that more drink could be consumed. The only other time the makeshift village was functional was at carnival, when there was a prize for whoever ran the booth which most accurately reflected the festive mood. Although this was independence, it appeared there would be no breaking with tradition, so as some secured their booths to the ground whole teams of helpers busily wired them for sound or flitted around with paintbrush in one hand, paintpot in the other, and helped dress the occasion with a certain style, enlivening the constructions with miniature flags of the new nation and other visual paraphernalia.

Bertram turned from this activity and walked across the street to the Ocean Front Bar. As he pushed at them the doors creaked, for the seaspray had finally rusted the hinges. He looked at the thinly-salted windows and noticed that the hinges had not been the only victims of the sea. But nothing else seemed to have changed. In the corner stood a piano that Bertram had always assumed to have once been a musical instrument. Small round drinking-tables were scattered liberally around the floor, each surrounded by exactly three chairs. And the tall stools at the counter, the stools they used to call American stools for they were like the ones they saw in the movies, they too were still there. Unlike the rum shops of the side streets and country villages, which often smelt thick with the scent of cane, and into whose dirt floors were crushed bottletops and bits of glass, the Ocean Front Bar had always maintained a certain style. Bertram was glad to see that this remained the case. He walked across the empty bar and slid up and on to a stool. At first Bertram thought he recognized the barman, but as the young man turned to face him he saw now that he was a stranger.

'I'll take a beer.'

'Foreign or local?' asked the barman. As he did so he snapped his towel, and a fly flew from the plastic case under which there were sandwiches, veterans of the establishment.

'Local, please.'

The man turned and opened the freezer. He pulled a bottle-opener from his back pocket and Bertram saw that it was attached to his belt by a piece of string. Then he opened a bottle and placed it in front of Bertram.

'You want a glass?'

Bertram studied the label with great interest. Again the man asked him if he wanted a glass, and this time Bertram looked up.

'No, thanks.' He paused. 'I didn't know we start making our own beer.'

'Well, you know now,' said the man as he began to clean the top of the counter with a soapy rag. Bertram lifted the beer to his mouth and drank. It touched his stomach like petrol on live ashes, and he glowed inside. The man wiped the space where the bottle had been, then wrung out the cloth into a bowl.

'So how long it is since you been away?'

'Twenty years or so,' said Bertram, feeling rather foolish that he was imparting this information to a man so much younger than himself.

'Well, we had our own beer for nearly ten years. In fact I think it might even be eleven. We had a tenth anniversary last year if I remember right.'

He turned and looked off towards an open door, which Bertram knew led to a kitchen area. He shouted:

'It's last year we had the brewery anniversary?'

There was a short pause, then a woman's voice darted back sharp and clear. She sounded annoyed, as though she had been interrupted in the middle of doing something important to answer this foolishness.

'Of course it's last year!'

He turned back to Bertram.

'Seems like it's eleven years since we had our own beer now.' He stopped, then tossed his head in the direction of the woman's voice. 'I was due to marry to she but when I discover how much mileage she have I offer her a job instead.'

Bertram assumed he was supposed to laugh, but the man went on.

'Anyhow, that still don't stop her cutting into my conversation like a blasted Spanish radio station all day and all blasted night.'

'I see,' said Bertram, unsure as to how to respond, and now keen to change the topic of conversation. 'And what happen to the old man, Denton?'

The barman straightened up and wiped his wet hands on the back of his pants.

'Well, old men don't live for ever, you know. They must die like the rest of us, only old men seem to do it faster.'

'It seems so,' said Bertram, 'but it's a shame for Denton was a good man. He used to give me my first shots of dark rum, then bit by bit he weaned me on to the hard stuff, the Hammond. I taking rum like a man under his guidance.'

Bertram paused, as though thinking of a suitable epitaph, then he simply shook his head and raised his bottle in a toast to absent friends. The barman picked up his own bottle from behind the counter and joined him.

'Denton was my father,' said the barman as he put down his beer.

Bertram looked at him and saw now why he thought he recognized the man when he first walked into the bar. He had the same bow-tie shaped nose, and his ears were large, which made Bertram wonder why he did not wear his hair a little longer as his father had done.

But, like Denton, he had a self-assurance that despite his small and compact stature, immediately precluded the possibility of anyone ever taking liberties with him.

'I'm proud to meet you,' said Bertram.

He stretched out his hand and the young man pumped it spongily, for his grip was still slightly damp from his cleaning.

'I'm Lonnie.'

Bertram smiled and nodded. 'And you must call me Bertram.'

The man took a drink then spoke once more.

'So you coming in from England?'

He asked the question confident in the knowledge that Bertram did not have an American accent.

'I been living there since I left.'

'And how you finding England? Cold, I bet.'

'Cold, for sure,' said Bertram. 'But it has its benefits. Plenty of black people there so you never really getting out of touch.'

'Me, I been to Puerto Rico once for holiday, but I never been to England. I don't think I will like it though, any more than I like Puerto Rico.'

Bertram laughed. 'Perhaps one of these days I'll check out Puerto Rico, and maybe America itself.'

'You're welcome to it. A next drink?' asked Lonnie, noticing Bertram's empty bottle.

'Sure, why not?'

Bertram passed him the old bottle and watched as Lonnie reached for the new one.

'I wonder if you notice any other changes besides the beer since you reach back?' Lonnie placed the bottle in front of Bertram, but gave him no time to answer. 'You notice both the fire-station and the library burn down?'

Bertram raised his eyebrows. 'The fire-station?'

'Yes, man, the damn fire-station burn down too. It make you wonder what kind of a place we living in.'

Bertram nodded and took a swig from the new bottle of beer. Then he cleared his throat, but Lonnie went on. 'And what else? Owner-trash is still owner-trash, a funeral director and a doctor gone into partnership to open a rum distillery so they can both have more business, and our finest minds, the lawyers, the doctors, the odd businessman, who all been overseas to study and come back, are so bored with how easy it is to make money off the back of the people that they getting drunk for kicks and betting on who can lap up the most sewage water from the gutter.'

Again Bertram was unsure as to how to respond. In the end he decided to nod quickly, and say something before Lonnie could continue.

'Tell me,' he asked, 'does Jackson Clayton come in here at all?'

'Jackson Clayton comes in here every day for his lunch. He sits over there in the corner, and it's he who read the address at my father's funeral.'

Bertram felt satisfied with the information. Then he realized that he had better explain his enquiry to the young man, who was looking at him as though he had been cheated in this exchange.

'Jackson Clayton and I were best friends up until when I left the island.'

The barman nodded, ready now to proffer more information. 'He's a big man, you know. Some say when the Doctor resign the Premiership, if he ever resign that is, Minister Clayton bound to take over as the new leader.'

'And what do you think?'

The young man paused and looked at Bertram before venturing to answer. When he finally opened his mouth Bertram knew that the diplomacy and hesitation that enveloped each word meant that the man had not been able to make up his mind whether or not to trust him.

'I think Jackson Clayton is a very capable man.'

Bertram looked at him. Lonnie could see that he had not said enough so he went on. 'I'm sure that when he does take over the reins of this country that he will make a very significant impact on the situation.'

Bertram knew that his new friend was worried about what he had just said so he smiled at him, hoping that this might relax him. His friend smiled back.

'So how long you think Jackson going be today?' asked Bertram.

The young man studied his watch.

'Mr Clayton can be here any time in the next half an hour or so. You want to wait for him?'

'I'll wait for him over in the corner.'

'OK, OK. You want to walk with a next beer?'

'No, man, this one going do just fine.'

Bertram picked up his beer and wound his way around the small forest of tables to the one furthest from the counter. He sat with his back to the door and began to drink and think about his childhood friend. By the time he felt the hand drop on to his shoulder the bottle was empty. The voice was deeper than before, and a little more abrupt, but there was no doubt that it was that of Jackson Clayton.

'Excuse me, my friend, but this table is reserved so why you don't just take up any one of the other ones?'

Bertram stood up before he turned around, sure that this performance would draw from Jackson an even greater exclamation of surprise. But when he turned around Jackson's face was unmoved.

'Hello, Jackson.'

Jackson continued to look at him, the tumblers of his mind turning and trying to unlock the secret of this man's identity. Then the rattling in his brain ceased, and Jackson's mouth opened. His teeth were perfect, evenly spaced, media-white. Jackson's hair was cropped short in order to draw attention from the fact that he was balding, and his stomach was enjoying its last days of tightness. Jackson would soon have to tuck it in with his shirt.

'Jesus Christ, Bertram frigging Francis.'

'Right second time,' said Bertram.

'Good God, man, I was sure this independence would wash up all kinds of offshore troublemakers, but Bertram Francis. I swear to God I never did think I would see you again.'

Jackson opened his arms, and the two men folded neatly into one another's embrace. Then Jackson laughed and took a step back.

'You haven't changed a damn bit, man. The same lean kind of skinny Bertram, except somehow I did always picture you with a moustache.'

Now it was Bertram's turn to laugh, and he ran his eyes up and down the length of Jackson's body. Jackson shook his head and took a seat. Bertram resumed his place and they continued to look at each other.

'So you come home for good, or you just passing through or what?'

'Well, I come home for good, I think. If the island will take me, that is. Maybe I have to go back to England and sort out some affairs, but I'd like to open a business here so I must talk with you about investment opportunities.'

Jackson looked thoughtful. 'Well, you choose about the worst time for that kind of talk. Things really picking up now and swinging down towards independence so my time is kind of limited.'

Jackson could see the look of disappointment on Bertram's face.

'But I'll tell you what I'll do,' he said. 'Why you don't come and check me tomorrow, about three o'clock in my office, and I'll see if I can't dig up some information and some help for you then.'

Bertram looked pleased, and Jackson made a note of the appointment in a small diary.

'So,' said Bertram, 'I see you really making it now.'

Jackson pushed the diary back into his jacket pocket.

'Things have been lucky for me,' said Jackson as he signalled to the barman for the menu. 'I seem to keep falling on my feet while a few of the people around me keep landing on their arse. Nothing more complex to it than that.'

Bertram laughed, though he remained unconvinced by Jackson's flippant analysis of his success. Then Lonnie arrived and passed them both a thin dog-eared piece of paper which had every day's menu scrawled upon it in faded pencil.

'I'm taking chicken and a beer,' said Jackson, tossing the menu down on to the table top. Bertram looked up from the menu and passed it back to Lonnie.

'I going take the same. Why not?'

Lonnie walked back towards the counter, and Jackson and Bertram both listened as he shouted their orders off into the kitchen. Then Jackson coughed. He let his smile fade as he prepared to speak.

'I'm sorry about Dominic, man. It was a real shame for everybody like him. He kept his nose clean and worked hard.'

Bertram did not want Jackson to know that he had only just found out, so he dropped his eyes. There was a short pause in which Bertram tried to find the right tone of voice.

'I suppose I'm going to miss him. At first in England I couldn't do anything without wanting to tell him about it. I couldn't get used to his not being with me. He used to write these long letters, but I never was a good one for keeping in touch.' Bertram paused. 'He used to write a lot about his cricket and things.'

'They rob him of a place on the island team saying he do drink and womanize too much, and that he don't like to train.' Jackson spoke quickly then paused. 'He never did have any luck in the sports department.'

Bertram looked up at Jackson, unable either to imagine or believe in an adult and womanizing Dominic. In Bertram's mind Dominic had never developed beyond sixteen, and now he would never do so. Bertram dropped his eyes and spoke again.

'I just hope there wasn't too much pain or anything.'

Jackson seemed anxious to dispel this idea from

Bertram's mind. 'Well, I don't be no doctor, but as far as I can make out the car catch him as he walk out the factory and bragadam! that was it.' He paused. 'The fellar didn't stop, but Dominic was dead by the time they take him to the hospital.'

'You mean they never catch the driver?' Jackson shook his head. 'But there was bound to be some kind of indentation on the car!' protested Bertram.

'I know what it is you're saying, but they never catch anyone for it. The man must have hammered out the dent so his vehicle can pass for nearly any other car on the island.'

There was a silence. Then Jackson picked up the conversation on a different note. 'That's my sideline, you know. I sell cars and spare parts. Japanese cars, but built in the States and shipped down here. It's too far for us to keep having the British ones sent over, and besides you spend too much money ordering off to England for the spare parts. It don't be making any kind of sense any more.'

Bertram said nothing, for his thoughts hung knotted in his mind. Then Lonnie arrived and put the two plates of chicken and rice in front of them, and the bottles of beer to their side. Jackson soon turned from running off his mouth to filling his stomach, and Bertram began to pick at his meal in silence. At one point Bertram looked up, feeling sure that his friend's eyes were upon him, but he was mistaken. Bertram watched and noticed that Jackson's temples undulated as he ate. Then Jackson looked up and smiled at Bertram, who smiled back. Then they both continued their meal as though strangers.

At the top of the hill stood the church. The graveyard littered the hillside, and the many tablets of stone were of variable and independent design. Some looked old and worn, some brand new, some tall and statuesque, others squat and stubby. At the foot of the hill, and beyond these tablets, lay the schoolyard. In the centre of the schoolyard stood a small hut which was the school Bertram had attended as a child. Today both school and schoolyard were empty. Bertram watched as a distant car raced around the corner, then rode the afternoon heat-waves and journeyed on towards the capital.

Dominic's grave was modest and bereft of flowers. The simple name, Dominic Francis, was inscribed on a flat stone, but there were no dates to suggest either a breadth or a depth to his life. Bertram sat wearily on the edge of his brother's tomb. From where he sat Bertram could also see his father's grave, a man he had spoken about with his brother just the once. Bertram could have been little more than eight years old, which meant Dominic would have been five. And as they walked to school that morning Dominic had kicked at a stone, then stopped suddenly as though his body could no longer contain the question that was ready to burst from it.

'Somebody said they saw our father. Have you heard anybody talking about him?'

Bertram stopped and looked at his younger brother. With the outside of his sandal Bertram carved a neat line in the dusty road.

'Who told you this?'

'Lionel,' said Dominic. Then he looked up at his older brother, as if frightened that he had said something he was not supposed to know. Bertram looked back at him and then wandered on. Dominic followed and soon caught up with him.

'Tell your friend Lionel that he don't know what he's talking about,' said Bertram.

'So our father's not here?'

Bertram walked on, an eight-year-old boy grappling with adult considerations. Then he stopped.

'I think our father is in the hospital.'

'How long has he been there?'

Bertram looked at his younger brother knowing full well that he could not give him an answer based on fact. But he knew that to give him no answer at all would be far more damaging, so he quickly tried to think of something.

'I think he's only just arrived.'

'From where?' His brother looked up at him and Bertram was forced to carry on.

'I think he was in America doing some work but he's had to come back now.'

'Doing what work? And why did he come back now, why didn't he come back sooner?'

The tone of desperation that had crept into Dominic's voice frightened Bertram. His task now was to make his younger brother feel more at ease.

'I don't know why he didn't come back sooner. I'll have to ask Mummy.'

'If she was going to tell us anything she would have told us by now.'

Bertram could not dispute the logic of his brother's words, so he turned and walked on. Up ahead he saw some friends from his class so he tried to catch them. Dominic followed, a few steps adrift. Eventually Bertram realized that he was lost between his friends and his brother, so he slowed and waited for Dominic to catch up with him.

'I thought you didn't want to talk to me any more.'

Dominic was clearly upset.

'Listen, there's nothing we can do,' said Bertram, 'unless you want to go to the hospital and see for yourself.'

Dominic looked at him in a manner which indicated that this was exactly what he wanted to do. Bertram said no more. He draped his arm around his brother's shoulders and walked with him the rest of the way to school.

That afternoon they did not go back to Sandy Bay. Bertram arranged to meet with Dominic under the mango tree by the school entrance. Then together they took the bus to town, the pair of them still dressed in their brown and cream school uniforms. The William N. Williams hospital was at the near end of Baytown so they did not have to go down into the capital itself. They got off the bus and walked up the curved crescent towards the low white building, one of the few that had been constructed in concrete and glass, thanks to the generosity of a Canadian company which was trying to do a little for all the islands of the Caribbean.

A man in a rumpled black suit sat listlessly at the gate. As he wheezed they listened, and it sounded as though his nostrils were full of iron filings. His hair spiked angrily away from his scalp, and his head was gnarled like a root vegetable. Every few seconds it would snap forward as if about to fall into his lap. Bertram kept his distance and wondered if the man was a patient. Then the man growled: 'So where it is you two boys think you're going then?'

'We've come to see our father,' said Bertram, assuming the role of the elder statesman. 'He's in the hospital here.'

'He is?' said the man, as he now sat up a little straighter.

'Yes, he is.'

The man reached under his chair, pushed aside a crumbling Bible and picked up a brown folder. Then he looked at the two boys.

'Now then, what's his name?'

'Mr Francis,' said Bertram.

'Mr Francis,' repeated the man. 'Mr what Francis?' he asked, as he began to draw his forefinger down the list of names in front of him. Bertram did not answer so the man lifted up his head from the folder and looked quizzically at him.

'Mr what Francis?' he asked again. 'He must have a next name besides Mr Francis.'

'I don't know it,' said Bertram. He looked across at Dominic, who seemed as though he would cry if the man asked them any more questions.

'You don't know your own father's name?'

Bertram looked back at the man.

'Well, what does your mother call him?' The man placed the folder on his knees. Again Bertram turned to Dominic, who was obviously going to be of no help in this situation.

'She calls him Father,' said Bertram. He knew that this could not be right, but it was the best he could think of at the moment.

'Look, fellars, I can't see no Mr Francis on file so just tell me which one of you does favour your father's looks and I'll see what I can do for you.'

There was a long pause in which Bertram said nothing, and the man's head began to snap forward with even greater elasticity.

'Well, come on,' said the man, 'one of you must favour him.'

Bertram turned to his brother, but Dominic had already begun the long curved walk that would lead him back down to Island Road.

'Listen, man, you fellars making joke with me?'

'It isn't a joke!' shouted Bertram. 'And if you looked better I bet you you'd see our father's name down there, I bet you!'

With that Bertram chased off after Dominic. He caught up with him in the neck of the bend, and together they walked down to Island Road.

'You disappointed?'

Dominic nodded. Bertram knew he need say no more for his brother's eyes were full of tears which were ready to spill out.

When they reached Sandy Bay they saw their mother waiting for them at the top of the ghaut. As they walked down Whitehall she looked from left to right, right to left, clearly concerned about where the two of them could have got to. When Bertram saw his schoolfriends playing in their raggedy clothes, and he looked and saw what he and Dominic were still wearing, it made him realize why his mother seemed so agitated. She saw them both shortly after they had spotted her, but she did not wait for them to reach her. She simply turned on her heels and disappeared down the ghaut. As the two boys turned into the ghaut they saw her turn right into the yard.

'She's mad with us, isn't she, Bertram?'

Dominic began to cry.

They passed through the gate and made their way around the back of the house. Their mother stood outside the small kitchen pouring some soup from a large pot into a bowl for the dog to lick up. They both knew they would go hungry this evening. Frightened to say anything in case it precipitated the vexation they could see bubbling inside her, they went into the house and stripped off for bed, despite the fact that the sun had not yet set, and they could still hear the voices of their friends playing in the surrounding yards. Their mother did not come into the house, and when they heard the gate clang they assumed she had gone to visit one of the neighbours. They now felt free to talk.

'Do you think he's in there?' asked Dominic.

Bertram paused for a moment, but he knew exactly what he was going to say. After all, Dominic's friend Lionel was not the only one with the 'knowledge' that their father was on the island. Bertram had heard so for himself, and he was just as anxious as Dominic to find out the truth.

'I think he is,' said Bertram. 'But if he's in there he must be really sick.'

'Maybe he's going to die?' suggested Dominic. There was a long silence before Dominic continued. 'We can't let him die without seeing us.'

'Maybe he don't know who we are,' countered Bertram.

'But I still want to see him,' said Dominic. 'I just want to look at him.'

After this Dominic was quiet. Then some time later Bertram listened as his brother's breathing became both heavier and more regular. He was sure now that Dominic was asleep, so he settled down and waited for his mother to come home. He had made up his mind that he must ask her about their father, but when Bertram woke up it was morning and a cock was crowing. It would soon be time to nudge Dominic and prepare for school, and Bertram was annoyed that he had missed his chance to clarify the awful mess of their father.

And now, as Bertram sat on his brother's tombstone and looked across to that of his father, he thought of the only time his mother had ever mentioned their father. It was about six months later, and both he and Dominic had noticed that she had been very quiet with them for a couple of days. When she had people to the house she tended to talk in a whisper, even with people they knew and who could not by any stretch of the imagination be considered strangers. Bertram and Dominic both knew that something was wrong.

Then one morning she sent Dominic on ahead to school, and informed Bertram that she would like him to help her carry some water from the standpipe to the kitchen.

'But I'll be late for school,' protested Bertram.

'Just tell the teacher why you're late,' she said, 'and when I see him I'll explain to him myself.'

A reluctant Bertram picked up a pail and made ready for what he was sure would be half an hour of purgatory. But as soon as Dominic had passed out of sight his mother ordered him to sit back down and put the pail to one side. She said she wanted to talk with him. Bertram bunched up his knees under his chin, and then he squinted into the sun as he turned to face his mother.

'Bertram, I feel you're old enough to know that today your father is coming to Sandy Bay.'

Bertram felt a shock pass through his body, as though someone had struck him. His mother must have noticed for she rushed into her next sentence. 'Well, it's maybe not as you think for your father is dead.'

Again Bertram felt a shock, but this time he knew he would feel the effects of it for much longer.

'Shortly before Dominic was born your father left to go work in America.'

She stopped and looked at her eight-year-old son, worried that she might be asking him to take on too much knowledge too early. But Bertram seemed calm.

'You see he was a wild type of man, but he didn't disappoint me for I knew what sort of a man he was. A few months ago he came back for he had an illness which meant he needed to rest up. But now he's dead. I want you to know from me before you hear any kind of nonsense from anybody else. He was a good man, and this morning I'm going to go to his funeral and I would like you to come with me.'

She paused, but Bertram was unsure if he was expected to say anything so he kept his mouth shut.

'Would you like to come?'

Bertram nodded, then looked at his mother and saw that he was definitely expected to contribute something more substantial to the conversation.

'Yes, I want to come.' Feeling bold at this intervention, Bertram carried on. 'But can't Dominic come too?'

'Dominic is too young. He won't understand.'

Bertram listened to his mother knowing that he was not going to argue, but also knowing that his mother was wrong in her underestimation of the perception of her second son.

It was a dull, rather breezy day as the pair of them walked hand in hand up the hill towards the church. He noticed that adult eyes were upon him, eyes which now seemed uneasy at having to admit to their well-concealed knowledge of his father. But Bertram did not mind, for he was simply glad it would soon be over and he would be able to tell Dominic the truth.

Father Daniels conducted the short service. Then he made the discreet signal for the two men to come forward and start filling in the grave. For the first time all morning Bertram felt upset, and tears welled in his eyes at the thought of never knowing what his father looked like. With every clattering shovelful the chances of his ever being able to picture the man receded, and Bertram buried his face in the large folds of his mother's skirt and wished that he was somewhere else.

Now Bertram rose from his brother's grave. He thought they might have placed him a little closer to their father, but he realized that had they done so it would only have served to increase his feelings of guilt. For Bertram had never told Dominic of their father, and of the events of that day. It was not because his mother had forbidden him to do so, that alone would never have prevented him telling Dominic. It was just that Bertram felt he had colluded with her and deceived his younger brother, and to have talked about the funeral would have been admission of this. He now felt relieved that Dominic lay where he did, and their father some distance away. Bertram turned from the graveyard and began to walk back the half-mile or so to Sandy Bay.

He took the fork in the road and entered Whitehall, which was almost empty. Bertram assumed most people to be in Baytown now that Independence-ville had opened, and he walked on fearing recognition from the few who remained. All he wanted to do was return home and talk with his mother. As he passed by Leslie Carter's shop he risked calling out a casual 'Hello'. Mr Carter looked up from his counter and stared at him as though he could see some dreadful change that England had wrought in him. Bertram quickened his step and wished that he had kept his mouth shut.

The ghaut was deserted, but unlike the rest of the village it still felt pregnant with unseen activity. As Bertram tripped lightly over and in between the water pipes and broken bits of stone, he saw only scampering fowls. He pulled his shirt away from his body and realized he would have to get changed when he went in. He was still unused to the heat and perspiring abnormally like a tourist.

As the gate closed behind him Bertram heard voices. He walked around the back of the house and stopped. At the top of the steps was a woman he recognized as Mrs Sutton, though he could not be sure that it was her. She seemed smaller and more feeble than the woman he remembered teaching him in Sunday School. In those days her stomach used to grow in rubbery folds, and her forearms were overripe and flabby. Now she was shrunken, and the loose fat fell off her arms like bats hanging from a tree. She turned to face him and starfished her hands.

'Lord Jesus have mercy, is that really you, Bertram? It's really you come back after all these years?'

Bertram stared up at her as she continued.

'You know none of us ever expect to see you come back after so long, but you're not looking too bad considering.'

Bertram smiled, knowing that she had paid him a compliment meant only to remind him of who he was. And he looked at her, determined to avoid any conversation which might mean his having to justify himself.

'Since your brother gone, God rest his soul, I been coming down to help your mother out from time to time.'

She stopped, and looked at him as though wanting him to share a secret. Bertram looked back at her but was unclear as to what it was she might be trying to tell him. She saw this and turned from him. Bertram listened as Mrs Sutton now addressed his mother.

'I going drop by and see you tomorrow, alright?'

Bertram imagined his prostrate mother nodding back her reply.

'Now you just watch yourself. Anything you need just ask Bertram, and don't be trying to do too much.'

Bertram looked around at the kitchen and saw that the dog was no longer there. Then he heard Mrs Sutton slowly tiptoeing her way down the three steps and into the yard.

'Come,' she said. 'You can escort me back up the ghaut to my house. You seen the new place I'm living in?'

Bertram smiled and nodded. 'It seems very handsome to me. Just the sort of place you deserve after all these years.'

Mrs Sutton looked pleased and took his arm. Then she pointed her stick toward the gate, indicating the way they should move off.

As soon as they started to trudge their way up the dusty incline, Mrs Sutton turned to look at him. 'Your mother's not in too good health, you know.'

Bertram looked back at her. He wondered why she was wasting her breath on telling him the obvious. Mrs Sutton went on. 'Your brother passing on so suddenly seemed to take the spirit from her.' She paused. 'And not hearing from you didn't do her much good either.'

'I didn't know about Dominic until yesterday.'

The sentence fell gracelessly from Bertram's mouth. Mrs Sutton stopped and unhooked her arm.

'Bertram, you're talking to me like you're making a courtroom speech. It's the duty of the son to keep in contact with his mother. It's not for her to spend off money she don't have on postage and suchlike trying to track you down all over the place.'

Bertram bowed his head knowing full well that she was right. Then, after a cold stare, Mrs Sutton hooked her arm back into his, and again they began to make slow steps up towards the new house.

'You planning on staying for long?'

Bertram paused before answering, unsure of what it was this tiny woman was trying to ascertain. 'I don't know,' he said. 'I would like to come back here to live, but I have things to sort out that might take me some time.'

'What you mean?'

'Well, I have to live and work if I come back here, so I must make sure that I have means.'

'I see,' she said. 'But first I think you should make sure that you look after your mother. She don't have nobody else, and this may be your last chance to avoid a meeting with the man, Lucifer. You leave that brother of yours to bring her up and feed and clothe her in her old age, and since he gone it's me who have this responsibility.' She paused. 'Now don't get me wrong. I don't want you to think I won't keep doing so if you take it upon yourself to sling your hook again, but you better start thinking about your responsibilities. It's all well and good you gallivanting off all over the place, but you don't look to me like no young man no more and you soon going know what it's like to be old and dependent upon the kindness of other people.'

They were now at the top of the ghaut. Mrs Sutton stopped, and again she unhitched herself from Bertram. She pushed open her gate and went through.

'A big man like you must act big, and I'll be watching out to make sure that you do so. Your mother's a good woman and the fruit don't fall far from the tree.'

With this Mrs Sutton began to shuffle her way across the orange gallery. Bertram waited until she had passed out of sight and into the house before turning to make the return trip. It was only when he reached half-way down the ghaut that Bertram remembered he should have asked after her husband.

Once back at his mother's house he went to sit on the edge of her bed. He could smell a mustiness, which he took to be his mother. Then he felt the coldness of his shirt as a damp patch caught his body, and it occurred to him it might be he who smelt. His mother looked at him, her face revealing nothing, so he did not know whether she too could smell his body. She looked tired, her eyes dull as though clamouring for sleep, and Bertram tried hard to clear his mind of Mrs Sutton's words which still echoed ominously around his head. He had not yet thought of the new responsibility for his mother which now lay with him, and as he looked at her he tried not to begin to think of it now. After twenty years he had already discovered that he still felt an attachment to the house, and to the village, and to his mother, but as much as it shocked him to have to admit it, the attachment he felt towards his mother was in no way greater than that he felt towards these other facets of his life that he thought England had stripped from his consciousness.

'I went to Dominic's grave.'

Bertram knew he would have to begin whatever conversation it was they might have. His mother continued to look at him, but she said nothing. Then she closed her eyes.

'Your brother missed you. He never grew to hate you, he just missed you as we all did to start with. Then some of us grew used to the fact that England had captured your soul, but he didn't. For Dominic you were always coming back.'

'And now I'm back.'

His mother opened her eyes.

'And now you've been to see him.' She paused. 'I don't want to talk about Dominic. The boy did his best to nurse whatever difficulties he had in his heart, but he was never the same once you did desert him. Eventually he just took up with a wrong set of people, but you could have helped prevent that.'

They fell together into a silence which was initially difficult, then seemingly impossible for them to arrest. Bertram felt sure it would have to be him who made the move to resume their dialogue, but to his surprise it turned out to be his mother who spoke first.

'You've been to see Patsy today?'

Bertram shook his head, mystified as to why she should ask such a question.

'I hope you see her before you leave.'

'I told you I want to stay and try and start up a business of some kind.'

'Yes, I remember, independent of the white man.' His mother stared at him with scornful eyes. She went on, 'You know as yet what kind of a business it is you're hoping to get involved in?'

'I saw Jackson Clayton today. Remember Jackson?'

His mother's look said everything about the stupidity of his question. Bertram continued, 'Well, I have a meeting with him tomorrow about what opportunities there are. He seemed quite optimistic.'

'He talk to you about Patsy?'

Bertram shook his head.

'I think the least you can do is go and see her for once upon a time she deafen your ears with love and have you cock-walking around the island like you own the place. As for him, he did spoil. First his personality begin to crack up, then bleed, and when his first success arrive he just start to spurt blood on anyone who comes near him. He's no good now.'

Bertram took his mother's hand and let the silence drift. Her insistent references to Patsy disturbed him, but they also made him determined to avoid any further discussion of her. He tried to shift the conversation back to the events of the day, and find out why she talked about Jackson in such disparaging tones.

'I know it's going to be hard to find the business opportunities I'm trying to pin down, but I feel Jackson can help.'

His mother looked at him in a different way now. A more penetrating way, and Bertram realized there was also a certain bitterness etched across her face.

'I don't really care how hard or how easy things is going to be for you, Bertram, for no matter how hard you might think they be, they can't be no harder than you make it for Dominic and myself when you abandon us here and go about your own selfish matters in England.'

Bertram looked at her and spoke quietly, feeling obliged to defend himself.

'I couldn't come back.'

His mother slipped her hand out of his.

'What do you mean you couldn't come back? You ignore the boy's letters to you, then the man's letters to you. Somebody lock you up over there or what?'

'Nobody lock me up.'

'Then why the hell you couldn't come back to your own family, just tell me that? Why it is that you being so damn secretive about the whole thing? Even to this very minute you still don't have the decency to tell me what happened in England.'

'Nothing happened,' said Bertram, skirting the edge of an argument. 'I just couldn't study the course so I took work and one thing led to another. To me it just seems like two or three years, not twenty.'

'Bertram, I look foolish to you?'

'But it's the truth,' he said. 'England just take me over. New things start to happen to me, new people, like I was born again and everything is fresh. But it's only today walking about Sandy Bay and Baytown that I can see that maybe I was born again the same fellar. Nothing happened to me in England, you can believe that? A big rich country like that don't seem to have make any impression on me. I might as well have left yesterday for I just waste off all that time.' He paused. 'I think I'm the same fellar.'

His mother continued to look at him, but still she said nothing.

'I don't have no excuse for not writing for so long and falling out of touch, but you can't let me try and make it up now that I find the courage to come back?'

'And this is all you have to say?'

Bertram sighed. 'It's all there is. I really don't know where to start,' he pleaded.

'Well, you don't have to start no place for it is really causing you so much pain and trouble to get around to speaking with me on this subject then I don't want to know, and that's God's truth. I really can't be bothered to know, and I don't want you back here, Bertram, I really don't want you in my house for you done shame me enough and I can't take no more.'

'You don't want me in the house?'

His mother fixed a hard and resolute glare upon him. 'You can stay here the night, in fact you can stay here a few more days, then either you must go back to wherever it is you come from, or if you must stay on the island and mess up my life with your nonsense, you must find a next place to live, you understand?'

Bertram looked at her, unsure that she was speaking from her heart. He said nothing in the hope that she might change her mind, but as she stared at him her anger seemed to grow.

'You gone deaf as well, or maybe you think I like to talk to myself?'

'I understand you,' said a quiet Bertram. 'I'll leave you as soon as the independence day is over.'

'And where you going?'

Bertram stood up and made ready to leave the room.

'I don't know.' He paused. 'But I can find somewhere.'

'Well then, you better find somewhere.'

Clearly this was his mother's last word on this or any other topic. She rolled over, her infirm body beginning to palpitate as she did so, and presented her son with the back of her head.

Once in the other room Bertram took off his shirt and looked for somewhere to hang it. Then he realized it would make the room smell, but it was dark outside, a night of hidden eyes and strange noises, and he could not be bothered to go out and fill a bowl with water and soak the shirt. So he screwed it up into a small ball and pushed it into a paper bag. He scratched at his armpits, then drew a hand under and around them. He smelled, but he would have to smell until morning. He cleared a space on the settee-cum-bed, then he heard the high bugle of a mosquito as it darted past his ear. He lit a coil and lay down, and again he began to sweat profusely as the crickets commenced their evening anthem. Bertram looked backward, above his head and out of the window at a firefly that glowed like a red light against the sky. It dashed past, then back again, then it was cruelly swallowed up for ever by the blackness of the night. Then he tried to run through the order of the day's events. He saw Denton's boy, he saw Jackson, his brother's grave, his father's, then Mrs Sutton, and finally his mother. At the end of this day he found himself piecing together the confused happenings and attempting to marry them to the follies of his expectations. But his jumbled thoughts quickly distilled down to one overwhelming truth. Although he had felt a life back home in the country of his birth was worth struggling for, his mother had now made him unsure whether the trial was over.

Bertram slept badly, and woke with his mind full of the previous night's conversation. Not wishing to risk the awkwardness of another talk with his mother, he got up and pulled on a clean shirt. Then he stopped and realized that this morning he would have to take a wash. Bertram took off his shirt and opened the door to the day. He picked up a bowl and stepped down into the yard. Once at the standpipe he opened the tap and heard the rusty artery protest with a loud vibration. Then he watched as first a brownish trickle then clearer water splashed out. Bertram let it settle but it still buzzed with dirt. Having looked around to make sure that nobody was watching, he started to rub down his body. The sharpness of the cold water pricked his skin like blunted needles, but he felt better for it. He tipped away the water and stretched. Then Bertram discovered that he had already been dried by the sun's heat, and there would be no need for him to use a towel.

Once back inside the house he rifled through first one suitcase, then the other until he found an even lighter shirt. The morning was already hot and he could not bear the thought of enduring another day in damp discomfort. His deodorant was useless, it seemed to evaporate within minutes of application, and having pulled on his new shirt he decided to carry with him a small bottle of aftershave to kill off any bad odours. Then he glanced at the clock and saw that it was only eight o'clock. But by Caribbean standards this was late and the day would already have begun. But then he remembered that today was a national holiday. Everything in his mind was so confused, but at least he still felt the elation of a new day which he hoped might offer something to erase the memories of the one just past. He went out to the kitchen and lit the stove, put on some water and made tea. Having drunk a second cup Bertram decided to leave in case his early-morning noises disturbed his mother. Before he did so he propped open the back door. It seemed highly unlikely that it would rain, and the fresh air circulating around the house would be essential if his mother was to sleep properly.

When Bertram reached the top of the ghaut he turned

left and began to amble along Whitehall in the direction of the pier. About six houses before the road ran into the steep hill which led down to the sea, a short path wound its way off to the right. Bertram followed it, side-stepping the raw-boned children who ran wildly up and down its length screaming like their parents' poultry. The noise in this narrow alley was much louder than in the rest of the village. In fact, the houses were so close to each other it was as if one large conversation was taking place. But distinguishable this morning, above both human and animal voices, was the cracking of small pieces of wood as they were slapped violently against a table top. The noise machine-gunned through the air as the unseen men continued to play dominoes.

When he reached the house Bertram stopped and felt a surge of relief. It was just as he remembered it, the same murky colour, the same obsolete outhouse, the same pieces of fencing missing. Bertram leaned over what remained of the fence and shouted. But as he did so he wondered if perhaps he was making a mistake. Too much had happened between the two of them for him to get English on her now. He should have casually sauntered into the yard and then shouted, but it was too late now. So he remained by the fence and shouted again.

'Patsy, you home?'

There was silence. Obviously everybody within ear-shot could hear, but nobody said anything. Bertram drew strength from this, for he knew that if she was out someone would have called to him. But he could not decide whether or not to shout a third time, feeling that his imported manners might be annoying the neighbours. However, a decision proved unnecessary for at that moment she opened the door.

Patsy was dressed in a plain white shift, which fell dowdily from her shoulders. She rubbed her eyes, then shielded them from the sun as she tried to focus on Bertram. But he could see her quite clearly. Her shift came down as far as her calves, and her feet were bare and spread wide. These days Patsy was small and podgy, as though she had been moulded in brown dough. She looked curiously peaceful, and as he looked at her Bertram remembered that one of the things he had found most appealing about Patsy was her tranquillity. People had always stared at her because she walked so slowly, so calmly, even in the teeming rain, but she never seemed to notice their eyes. In her chubby face, in her still short though now slightly plumper frame, Bertram could clearly recognize the childhood girl of his dreams and he smiled broadly.

Patsy's mouth dropped open. She stood rooted to the spot and stared at this man, who had arrived as though for a prearranged appointment.

'Bertram Francis?' Patsy whispered. She tried to refocus her eyes. 'Bertram?'

Bertram felt his already broad smile widening. He moved to his left and carefully uncoupled the latch on the gate. He fastened it back and walked across the small dusty yard and presented himself before her.

'My God, Bertram, you're alive and well. And you seem like you could pass for your old self.'

She carefully scanned him, his black leather shoes cleanly polished, his slacks neat and fashionable, his shirt light and sensible.

'I see somebody must be looking after you, but your neck is too high to wear collarless shirts.'

Bertram said nothing. He looked back at her and wanted her to go on speaking, but she had no more words. He watched as she slowly laced her arms around his neck, and he found himself slipping his around her waist and hugging her tightly.

'Let me just hold you, Bertram, and make sure it's really you come back.'

Bertram closed his eyes and brushed his chin against her closely-trimmed hair. The ease with which he fell back into her arms alarmed him, but at least someone had finally accepted him with unqualified joy.

'Excuse me, Miss Archibald, but my mother say to ask you if you have a yam for she to borrow.'

Patsy slipped Bertram's clinch and turned to face the small girl whose pants were threadbare, her legs powdered with dirt. She seemed nervous at having discovered Miss Archibald hugging this stranger, and she hopped from foot to foot.

'Just wait there a moment,' said Patsy, as she turned and disappeared inside the house.

'No school today?' asked Bertram. The girl shook her head. 'You looking forward to the independence?'

At first the girl looked down and shrugged her shoulders. Then she looked up and nodded fiercely as though anxious to correct herself. 'Yes, I'm looking forward to it.'

'Good,' said Bertram. 'So am I.'

The girl stared at Bertram as if begging him to terminate their conversation. Bertram smiled back having received her message.

Patsy reappeared carrying a single yam wrapped in a torn-off sheet of newspaper. As she walked towards him Bertram recognized the newsprint as that of the *Worker's Spokesman*.

'Now take this to your mother and tell her Miss Archibald say she going come by later and see how things is.'

The girl took the yam and slowly walked off. When she thought Miss Archibald and the man could no longer see her, she broke into a frenzied dash. Patsy turned back to Bertram.

'I see you looking hard at the paper? You read them since you return?'

Bertram shook his head.

'Well, you want to come inside and look at them?'

'I can wait,' said Bertram. 'I'm just curious to see how much things have developed, and how much is still as it was.'

'I see,' said Patsy.

'Maybe you can bring them out later,' suggested Bertram. 'I prefer to sit out in the sun. You can't believe how long it is since I seen the sun.'

'I know exactly how long it is since you last seen the sun,' said Patsy. She reached for a stool for him to sit on. 'I can count good.'

Bertram smiled and squatted on it, then he looked around and reacquainted himself with Patsy's almost ascetically empty yard. Then he turned back to Patsy.

'Your aunt dead?'

Patsy nodded.

'I'm sorry,' said Bertram.

'No need to be sorry. She was in pain for too many

years. For her death was a liberation. I feel she's probably better off now.'

Bertram continued to look at her, but he was unsure how to respond. There was a long silence. Her aunt had been bedridden for as long as Bertram could remember but to him it still seemed cruel to talk about the dead in this way, although he felt Patsy meant nothing by it.

'I'll get you those papers now,' said Patsy.

Before he had time to tell her not to bother, Patsy had passed into the house. She came out carrying a pile of newspapers, much as one would carry a new-born baby. She dumped them at Bertram's feet so they fanned out in disarray.

'You can manage by yourself for a few minutes?' asked Patsy. 'I have to go pick some fruit and see to some things down the road.'

'I can manage,' said Bertram, wondering to himself what Patsy imagined his status in her yard to be. He watched as she took up a basket and closed the door to the house. Then she walked past him, and Bertram noticed that her large breasts were no longer firm. As she moved they swung from side to side. Patsy opened the gate and turned around to face him.

'You seen Jackson since you come back?'

Bertram was waiting for her to ask this, so she did not catch him by surprise. 'I saw him yesterday, and I'm supposed to go down and see him again today about some business opportunities.'

'What business opportunities?'

'If I'm going to stay here I must have a way to earn my living and establish myself in some kind of comfort that don't rely upon the white man.'

Patsy looked puzzled. She was clearly surprised that Bertram was considering returning to the island for good. 'I suppose so,' she said. Then she turned and left, and Bertram switched his attention to the newspapers.

Their parochialism depressed him. Having read yet another story about corruption, this one involving the alleged theft of some fruit by a civil servant some thirty-two years ago, he threw them down. His mind drifted both backward and forward to Jackson, but this time he thought of Jackson in relation to the woman whose yard he now sat in.

Having captured the scholarship, and begun work at Vijay's Supermarket, Bertram devoted the greater part of his time to Patsy. The hours he had invested with Father Daniels over questions of English and History and Law were now spent with his girl. And instead of planning cogently for his future studies, he moved into what the *Worker's Spokesman* would have called a full-blooded carnal dotage upon her. But inevitably, as Bertram's fame increased – and his notoriety spread as he and Patsy became Sandy Bay's royal couple – his friendship with Jackson began to fall by the wayside. Although, of course, Bertram did not see it this way. As far as he was concerned he simply had less time to spend with everyone, including Jackson. But Jackson said nothing.

When there was little more than a month to go before Bertram's departure, Patsy began to show signs of irritation with him. Up until this point theirs had been a relationship with its own unchallenged momentum and little analysis of why it was they were together. One afternoon, after they had made love in a cove to the north of the broken-down pier, Patsy stood up and pushed her skirt down to just below her knees, where it hung naturally. Bertram watched her, then brushed the sand from his elbows as it was beginning to irritate his skin.

'So you decide as yet what is going to happen between the two of us?'

Bertram looked at Patsy, completely taken aback by the abruptness of her question. He had expected the subject to come up sooner or later, but he assumed she might have waited at least another week or so. However, now that she had brought it up, he began to compose himself in order that he might manoeuvre what he knew would be a difficult conversation.

'Me decide?' he asked, mustering as much innocence as he dared. 'Me decide what? What is there to decide?'

'About us, Bertram,' said Patsy, now turning to face him. 'Do you want me to put it to you bluntly? It's not hard to do.'

'What's not hard to do?'

Bertram heard the words before he could arrest them. Patsy now stared angrily at him.

'Are your intentions towards me honourable, Bertram?'

'What do you mean honourable?' asked Bertram, his voice breaking as he spoke. 'Do you think I want to do you some harm?'

'You know exactly what I mean. You're going away for three years, maybe more, and it's you that spoil me so I want to know if it's me you're intending to marry.

Or maybe you waiting till you get to England to look a next woman?'

Bertram stood up and tucked in his flapping shirt. The ferocity of her attack was taking him by surprise, and he needed more time to prepare himself. But Patsy gave him no time, and again she turned on him.

'Well, Bertram, you planning on marrying me when you return, or, if it's not going to embarrass you arriving in England with a coloured woman, maybe you're thinking of taking me with you?'

'Don't talk foolishness! You can't embarrass me in any place, and I've thought about taking you. But I must face the facts. How the hell can I support myself and a next person and get on with the task of studying? It just don't make no kind of financial sense.'

'I see, so you putting more emphasis on the financial sense than on someone you keep saying means more to you than anyone you ever met in your life.'

Bertram sighed, unable to believe the malevolence of the conversation he had now been dragged into.

'Patsy, three years is not a lifetime. When I come back we can just pick up where we left off. Things going be hard enough for me in England without taking you along as extra baggage.'

'As extra what?'

'You know what I mean.' A light sweat now broke out on his brow. 'Alright, so maybe I didn't say it sweetly but extra baggage is what it's going to be like in the end.'

'Well, in that case you won't be wanting any extra baggage waiting for you when you return.'

Patsy stared at him, letting him know that if he had anything to say it was now his turn to speak. But Bertram stared back at her and declined the offer. However, he eventually capitulated.

'Perhaps you can come and visit me in England before I return.' Her face was unmoved and she said nothing. 'Or maybe I might be able to get a job on the side and save up and come back for a short holiday before my time is up.'

Again she said nothing, and Bertram now knew he was being presented with Patsy's ultimatum. He searched in vain for a compromise, but in his heart he knew she had outflanked him. As he opened his mouth she spared him the indignity of gabbling.

'You better prepare yourself for going to England, Bertram.' Patsy paused. 'I think it's best if we don't see each other again, and that way we can both start our lives afresh, and maybe properly this time.'

As she walked away from him, Bertram followed her slender shape with his eyes, wondering if this really was the same woman whose body he had been enjoying only minutes before. He looked at her and tried to imagine that she might have a tear of regret in her eyes. This alone would go some way towards explaining her behaviour, but Bertram knew he was deceiving himself, for Patsy's premeditated assault had clearly been arranged so as to exclude the possibility of any emotional weakness.

Bertram stared out over the sea and into the distance. He looked at the easy arched movement of a solitary boat that rose and fell, and at the birds that seemed to glide for ever without beating their wings. Then he played a game with himself that he often did when disturbed. He would pick out a spot on the horizon, focus on it, then close his eyes and try and imprint it on his mind. Then he would reopen his eyes and look again, and try to pick out a spot beyond it, close his eyes, imprint, then open his eyes again and try to look even further beyond that spot. This way he was trying all the while to see further into the distance so that he might one day see another island that nobody else had ever seen, and then proceed to people it with persons from his mind so that he had his own world that nobody could touch. But he soon tired of his game, and as the sun began to slide down the back of the sky the reflected light on the water hurt his eyes. He brushed off more sand from his elbows, then began to walk up the hill towards Whitehall. He decided not to drop in on Patsy, feeling that she was probably expecting this of him. Tomorrow he would see her and try to make everything all right, but tonight he would go home and think.

In the morning Bertram called by Patsy's house, but there was nobody at home. Her aunt was still in the hospital so he assumed Patsy was visiting. Bertram walked back down the alley, along Whitehall, then down the ghaut to his home. He should have gone straight up to Island Road and caught the bus into Baytown for work, but he felt too depressed. He told his mother he felt ill, and she told him it must be the overwork and worry from the scholarship. She made him lie down, and assured him that she would get a message to Vijay's Supermarket. But Bertram did not sleep. He lay in bed upset and embarrassed at how quickly fortune could turn sour. He resolved to get up and write a note to Patsy, and once his mother had left the house, to go around and leave it by her place. But as he heard his mother slam the door, he changed his mind, fearful that one of the neighbours might tell his mother they had seen him on his feet. So he lay back and waited for Dominic to come back from school, which he did, only to ignore him as usual.

Bertram slept very little that night, but in the morning he got up briskly in order to convince his mother that he now felt better. She seemed pleased, and Bertram dressed quickly and left as though going to work. He went, however, straight around to Patsy Archibald's and called at her gate. But as he first stood, then leaned up against the fence he felt stupid, for the school-children stared at him as though they knew something of which he was ignorant.

''Morning, Bertram. What do you want?'

Patsy appeared in her nightdress and spoke civilly, but coldly. Bertram could see that he had just woken her up, and his first thoughts were of what it was she could have been doing so late that had kept her in bed for so long this morning.

'I just called to see if I can see you tonight?'

'You didn't hear what I said the other day?'

Bertram began to feel humiliated, and he wished he had not bothered to drop around.

'I heard what you said, but I thought if I came and talked to you that maybe we could come to some decision.'

Patsy fixed her eyes upon him, and as she did so she seemed to take on years beyond the nineteen she already possessed.

'Bertram, you had your chance to say whatever it is you feel about me. Why it is that you coming to see me just now?'

Bertram looked at her, unable to believe that he could have misjudged her character so completely. He stared until it became apparent that for his own safety of mind it might be wise if he said nothing further. So he pivoted and stopped only when he heard Patsy's voice again.

'Anyhow, Bertram, I can't see you now for to do so would be unfaithfulness.'

Bertram looked back at her.

'What do you mean unfaithfulness?' His voice soared. 'Why you don't stop playing games with me? What it is I done to you that suddenly turn you into this?'

'Well, for a start, Bertram, you just take and you use. In case you ever run into a next woman, you should be aware of what kind of a man you are, and the truth is you're the worst kind.'

Bertram felt himself being dragged back into the nightmare he was on the point of escaping. He turned and began to walk away for the second time, but again Patsy spoke and stopped him.

'I'm sure your friend Jackson ain't going just take me and use me.'

'Jackson?' said Bertram.

'Yes, Jackson,' confirmed Patsy. 'He ain't going off on no big scholarship, and he also happy to make an honest woman of me. He ask me to marry to him so you better make sure you ready to face that when you come back.'

Bertram stared at Patsy. At first he imagined her to be overjoyed with the news, but then he saw the look in her face did not carry so heavy a message. In truth she seemed nothing more than relieved, and he no longer felt angry with her as his thoughts now turned towards his supposed friend, Jackson. But the fact was that Patsy could not have been trapped by Jackson unless she wanted to be, so he could not direct his anger towards him any more than he could towards her. In the end he was just grateful that they had spared him the indignity of carrying on a relationship behind his back. Bertram continued to stare at Patsy. But she looked back, her eyes both derisive and apologetic.

When Bertram woke up the papers were littered at his feet like leaves from an autumn tree. He glanced up and saw a tall gangly boy in his late teens watching him with a curious mixture of indifference and fascination. His hair was relaxed and sheened in the manner of prominent black American entertainers, and from his neck dangled a pair of black wraparound sunglasses on a thin fashionable cord.

'Sorry, mister, I didn't mean to wake you up.'

Bertram crushed his hand into his face and tried to massage the sleep from his eyes.

'Don't worry,' he said. 'I think I was about to wake up anyhow.'

The boy leaned against the fence and scratched the wispy growth he imagined to be a beard.

'What time is it?' asked Bertram.

A large, but obviously cheap, Japanese watch adorned

the boy's otherwise naked arm. He turned slightly for the sun was catching the face of the watch and making it impossible to read. Then he announced the time. 'It's just after two.' He looked at Bertram and found the confidence to go on. 'Mister, I don't think you should sit out in the sun without your head covered up. I once see an English fellar catch sunstroke and it don't be no pretty sight.'

Bertram stood up. 'You're right,' he said. 'I've been away for so long that even the simplest things seem to be escaping my mind these days.'

The two of them looked at each other, then Bertram broke the silence.

'You come looking for Miss Archibald?'

The boy nodded.

'Well, I don't know where it is she gone off to but I expect she soon come back. I have to dash off myself.' The boy said nothing.

'Listen,' said Bertram, 'you going wait here for her?'

'I'll wait,' said the boy.

'Well, then, maybe you can do me a favour?'

The boy's look made it clear that he was not promising anything. Bertram went on.

'If you're still here when Miss Archibald comes back just tell her that Bertram Francis had to go to town, and maybe he'll see her later.'

The boy thought for a moment, then spoke. 'You're a delegate from overseas for the independence?'

'A delegate?' asked Bertram.

'You representing a country here? Maybe you can get me a job where you come from. I have some qualifications and I can work hard.'

Bertram watched as the boy struggled to check his enthusiasm.

'I'm not a delegate from anywhere,' said Bertram. 'So I'm not sure how I can get you a job.'

There was a long pause in which the boy now tried to disguise his disappointment.

'Have you met any delegates?' asked Bertram. The boy nodded.

'I work at the big Royal Hotel. It's where most of the foreign people and press and so forth are staying.' He paused. 'You look a little like a delegate which is why I asked you.'

Bertram nodded. 'And what work it is you do at the hotel?'

'I work in the gardens. I'm in charge of cleaning out the artificial lake.'

The boy was clearly proud of his job, so Bertram tried to look pleased.

'It seems like a good job to me. Why it is you're in such a hurry to leave?'

'I think I prefer America,' said the boy. 'New York Yankees, Washington Redskins, Michael Jackson, you can't want for more than that. The West Indies is a dead place.'

'How you mean dead?'

'I mean dead,' insisted the boy. 'Too small in size and too small in the head. I want to move on and up.'

'I see,' said Bertram, as he caught a glimpse of the boy's watch. 'Anyhow, I have an appointment in Baytown. So nice to meet you . . . ?'

'Livingstone,' said the boy.

'Nice to meet you, Livingstone. Maybe I'll come

down and see you at the hotel, so long as you don't mistake me for a delegate.'

Livingstone smiled. 'All delegates in the hotel must wear a special independence badge.'

'Well, you'll recognize me then, won't you – remember, no badge.' Bertram laughed nervously and walked out of Patsy's yard. He passed the strange boy who hovered now, as though preparing to mount an alert guard.

Once in Baytown Bertram was absorbed by the carnival atmosphere. All the booths were completed and people were drinking and dancing to the music. Bertram was tempted to go and join them, sure that he would meet up with a few contemporaries, but he disciplined himself and decided to put business first. Jackson might be an old friend, but he was now also a minister, and he had already made it clear that his time was precious.

Bertram was soon at the gates of Government House, where he found himself face to face with a man wearing a smart white uniform. Above them the sun burned its way through a cloud and further lit up what was already a bright day, and Bertram wondered if this might be a good sign for his meeting with Jackson. The man before him stood sternly erect and partnered a machine gun (a relic from the Second World War). He had a swollen, pock-marked face that had at some point in his life taken on an expressionless gaze and hardened like quick-drying plaster into a mask. It hardly seemed credible to Bertram that the safety of the Government could be entrusted to this one man.

'I must ask you to please state your business,' said the man.

Bertram answered him in as relaxed a manner as possible. 'I've come to see Jackson Clayton. I have to have a word with him about something.'

'About what, sir?'

'Private business.'

'You have an official appointment?'

All the while the man's eyes were focused on something in the distance. He seemed to take no account of the fact that the voice answering his questions was coming from a fellow human being. Bertram spun around to see what it was the man was looking at, but apart from Blakey's, the local bar-hotel that was owned by some Syrian immigrants, there was nothing and nobody in sight. Blakey's was an old colonial wooden building that appeared ready to fall down at any moment. As he turned back to face the man, it flashed through Bertram's mind that this architectural death might be just what the man was waiting for.

'I have an official appointment,' confirmed Bertram.

The man finally looked at him, as if unsure that he was being told the truth. Then he encouraged his eyes to harden back into a frustrated and distant glare.

'Go see the fellar in the window and tell him what it is you want.'

Bertram looked at the uniformed man, outraged by his lack of courtesy. However, he thought it politic not to say anything.

The man at the window reminded him of the man he had just left. He was young, but unlike the man with the gun he was not uniformed. He flicked carelessly through a crumpled copy of the *Worker's Spokesman*, and scratched at his hair. Bertram noticed that every time he did so he looked under his fingernails as though expecting to find something there. Behind him Bertram could see other civil servants sitting and talking, and one among them avidly reading a copy of *Playboy* magazine.

'I've come to see Jackson Clayton,' began Bertram.

'You have an appointment?'

''Course I have an appointment.'

The man looked up at him. Bertram carried on. 'I wouldn't come here if I didn't have an appointment.'

'Well, maybe you wouldn't,' said the man, 'for you're not from here and your people probably have a different way of doing things. But people here always trying all kind of damn foolishness to reach the ministers. Just wait while I see if Minister Clayton is expecting anyone.'

As the man picked up the telephone Bertram's eyes drifted back to the man in uniform. He was now stubbornly questioning yet another poor soul at the gate.

'You are Mr Bertram Francis?' asked the man at the window, his hand covering the telephone receiver.

'That's me,' said Bertram.

The man seemed to ignore this fact, and he returned to the telephone. Jackson now fixed his eyes upon the man's discarded newspaper. On the front page there was a large, but badly reproduced photograph of Jackson and the Doctor at a soil-breaking ceremony. The caption was neither story nor quotation.

This is a symbolic ceremony as we strive
to make this country self-sufficient. This
is not a Utopia. We cannot aim any lower.
The main products of this new enterprise will
be margarine and shortening, with room for
expansion into the reconstitution of butter.

(The blessing delivered by Father John
Martin of the Anglican Church.)

Eventually the man put down the telephone and pointed to the staircase. 'Go up to the third floor, turn left, then left again, and Minister Clayton's office is in the corner.'

Bertram kept his thanks to himself.

He climbed the open concrete staircase and wondered why the engineers and architects of the Caribbean had abandoned the cooler wooden buildings of his youth. He could now see that Government House was constructed in one large concrete square, with offices around the outside four walls and a courtyard in the middle. The courtyard was dominated by an ornamental pool decorated with artificial lilies, but the pool was open to the sky so that if it rained too much it would inevitably flood the ground-floor offices. That morning Bertram had read in one of the newspapers that there had been talk of draining the pool and filling it in with earth to make a small garden area. But then someone had pointed out that when it rained all the plants would drown and the ground-floor offices would probably still flood. At the next Beautification and Maintenance Sub-committee meeting the question of a roof was to be raised.

Jackson's secretary looked just as he imagined she would. Small, very pretty, and obviously totally under Jackson's spell. She sat at her typewriter and squinted up at the stranger. Then she reached for her glasses.

'Are you Mr Francis?'

Bertram nodded. She continued. 'Please wait a moment.'

She picked up the telephone, and in a lipstick-coated purr informed Jackson that his visitor had arrived. As she spoke she tried to keep the receiver covered, as though it was imperative that her conversation with the minister be secret. But Bertram stood right over her, which only served to accentuate her feelings of unease. He leaned forward and studied a large election poster that featured a photograph of Jackson, beneath which his credentials were impeccably listed.

The Honourable JACKSON CLAYTON, Deputy Prime Minister, Minister of Agriculture, Lands, Housing, Labour and Tourism

VOTE FOR THE MAN WHO

- Gives away half of his salary to Education
- Increased housing for low income families
- Increased food crop production in Agriculture
- Brought you the QE2
- Brought you Pan-Am
- Brought you Hollywood
- Introduced dull season bonus for sugar workers
- Increased assistance to fishermen

- Organized the first ever convention for East Baytown
- Is an ardent supporter of youth and sport in his constituency
- Keeps his promises

The secretary put down the telephone.

'Could you go in now, please,' she said, half-request, half-order. 'The Honourable Minister Jackson Clayton is happy to be receiving you, sir.'

'Thank you,' said Bertram, unsure if she was trying to sell him something.

Jackson was sitting behind his desk, head down, examining some papers. As Bertram walked in Jackson did not bother to look up.

'I'll be with you in a minute, Bertram. Take a seat.'

Bertram sat in the only available chair. He looked at the brown circle of skin that crowned the top of Jackson's head. Then he looked around the office. On the wall was a picture of Jackson in his cricket whites playing what looked to Bertram like a late cut. And to the side of this picture was a group portrait of the nine members of government. Bertram recognized two or three people from school. Then he recognized the Doctor, a bearded stubby man who affected a tweed-suited dignity which was little more than the aping of English mannerisms. Bertram imagined him to be one of those squat men who had their suits custom made, so that the trouser legs were not too long, and the jackets not too narrow.

'You been waiting long?' Again Jackson did not bother to look up.

'Well, I can't say I just march straight in here, if you know what I mean.'

'Well, nobody can just march straight in here. This is the seat of government and must be treated with some respect.'

Jackson threw down his pen and looked up.

'So who says I'm not treating it with respect?' asked Bertram.

'Nobody says so. I'm just telling you for you seem surprised that we keeping such a strict security. Anyhow, you well?'

'So-so,' said Bertram, surprised at the coldness of Jackson's reception. 'I thought maybe we could have a talk about what openings there might be for me here if I come back to live.'

Jackson looked closely at him, nodded slowly, then stood up. He walked around behind Bertram, deliberately trying to make him feel uncomfortable. As he did so Bertram hooked both feet around the bar of his chair.

'I see,' said the unseen voice. 'You want to know what opportunities there might be for you back here?'

Bertram, assuming the question to be rhetorical, sat still and remained silent, a client in a barber's chair.

'Well, let me put it this way,' said Jackson, the tone of his voice implying an almost perverse familiarity with power. 'What do you have to offer us? What is it about yourself that you think might be of some benefit to our young country?'

Bertram listened, unsure if Jackson was consciously parodying himself. Then, as Jackson stepped back around in front of him, Bertram realized that there was a swagger about Jackson's demeanour that belied any possibility of this being parody.

'What do you mean, what do I have to offer you?' asked a now tentative Bertram. 'You talking to me like I don't have anything to do with this place. I was born here, and I grew up here just like you.'

Jackson sat and leaned back in his chair, which gave way to accommodate such movements. And then he began to laugh. 'You have the wrong idea of the island, Bertram. You walking around thinking that nothing has altered, that nothing much is different, yet you can't see what is before your own eyes. You coming on like Father Daniels still got your head stuffed in your damn books. He make you go blind, or maybe it's something that happen in England that turn your mind so?'

Bertram looked back at him. 'I don't know what the fuck you're talking about, Jackson.'

The smile disappeared from Jackson's face. He leaned forward and spoke softly, as only a man completely sure of his own authority can do.

'I see, so you don't know what the fuck I'm talking about.' Jackson invested the word 'fuck' with an offensive stress, giving it an edge that Bertram had clearly not intended it to have.

'Look, Jackson, I just don't see what you're trying to say to me, that's all. Why you don't just talk straight and let me have it as clean as possible? Is there any business opportunities here for me to get involved in, or am I just wasting your time?'

'No, my friend,' said Jackson, his voice expanding as he became more sombre. 'It's not my time that you're wasting, it's your own.' They stared at each other, then Jackson went on. 'So tell me, Bertram, which is the closest major city to here?' Bertram looked emptily at him. A smile crept across Jackson's face. 'You don't know?'

Bertram kept his mouth shut, for he knew a trap had been set and he did not want to fall into it.

'It's Miami, not your precious London. Miami. You ever been to Miami, Bertram? You ever been to the States?'

Bertram shook his head, then he felt he needed to rescue the conversation from becoming a monologue. 'I've never been no place except England, and a day trip to France to buy some duty-free liquor.'

'You never been State-side?'

Bertram shook his head.

'Well, what you must realize is that we living State-side now. We living under the eagle and maybe you don't think that is good but your England never do us a damn thing except take, take, take. As for business opportunities, don't come sitting opposite me and thinking you can pull an easy route back into some cash for you don't even study the island as yet to see how things is. You barely back here and you wanting to invest in the place you remember, not the place that is. Take a walk around, see what you think of the island as it is today, see if you think you could live here, then come back and talk to me. You see what I'm saying?'

Bertram looked calmly at Jackson, but he could feel the perspiration breaking out on his palms and on the back of his hands.

'I can see that the island has changed for I'm not blind, you know. And I can see that more change is in the air, and independence only just around the corner and everything else. But this is my island too, Jackson, and just because you come minister gives you no right to talk down to me and try to make me feel small. I have a little cash and if I want to make a business here, right here where I was born, then nobody can stop me.'

Jackson laughed out loud.

'You think you, a little raggedy-arse boy who leave all this time ago, really carrying any swing around here?' He stood up and looked sympathetically at Bertram. 'Bertram, my old friend,' he began, 'if I want to make it so you can't have a business here I don't even need to raise my voice, let alone pick up a telephone. I can make it so damn uncomfortable for you that you going be better off taking a walk up Black Rocks and pitching off your money into the sea.'

Bertram stood, and with as much cool as he was able to muster, he leaned forward and faced his friend. He used Jackson's desk as a support.

'Thanks for your help, Jackson. Maybe I better just take a walk up by Black Rocks and pitch my money out into the sea.'

To his horror Bertram realized that as he spoke his voice kept fading, like a radio tuned in to a weak signal. He turned quickly to leave the room, but Jackson stopped him.

'Wait, Bertram. I'm telling you what I'm telling you for your own benefit. You think I'm getting any pleasure out of this?'

Bertram stopped and turned around. He could feel something inside of himself ready to burst.

'You really want me to fucking answer you that question, Jackson?'

Bertram opened the door and left. As he passed by Jackson's secretary she dropped her eyes and pretended to be occupied with her typewriter.

Out on the street the brightness made the shadows deeper, and what little shade there was hit Bertram like a cold shower. He realized he needed a drink, but rather than go down to the harbour and risk a conversation in the Ocean Front Bar or by one of the booths, he decided to wander into Blakey's. Behind the bar a girl listened to a crackly transistor blaring unnecessary warnings about Hurricane Hyacinth, which was now spinning tamely towards the Gulf of Mexico. She served him, but as she put down the bottle she spilled some and it stained the bar-top in a shape similar to that of one of the larger islands to the south. Bertram picked up his beer and moved to sit at a table which would give him a view out on to the street.

Of course the island had changed, he was not blind. There were bigger buildings, foreign vehicles, video shops, American news magazines on sale, a Pizza Hut, but all this was in the capital. Nothing much seemed to have changed in the country, but then he imagined that Jackson almost certainly lived in Baytown now and the differences that had always existed between country and town had simply become more marked. But for people like Jackson, a wealthier Baytown probably indicated a healthier island, despite the fact that the vast majority of the masses still lived in country poverty, a poverty that as far as Bertram could discern would only increase as long as agricultural workers were patronized in soil-breaking ceremonies by politicians who were saving up their money to buy yachts and even larger Japanese cars.

Bertram emptied the bottle in one and waved a thirsty hand at the girl. She moved at her own pace, but eventually she brought Bertram another beer.

'Two fifty, mister.'

She had a high, irritating voice, like a razor blade being drawn against a window-pane. Bertram gave her three dollars and told her to keep the change. The girl offered no acknowledgement of his generosity, but Bertram did not mind. He was simply grateful for a cold beer, and he tipped the bottle up to his mouth and once again looked out on to the street. The flurry of bikes and bells and car horns let him know that for those few who had to work the day was now at an end. The shops were closing down and the people moved off to escape the tropical languor, the women walking as though their hips were on swivel joints, the young men padding along on the balls of their feet, muscles like brown pears beneath their thin tee-shirts. Bertram turned his head and looked down an adjoining street where a boy was silently washing a car outside a verandaed house, his face closed and silent.

Bertram took two more beers in Blakey's. Then he decided to wind his way down towards the harbour area and take a quick drink in Independence-ville. As he walked the occasional rat hurtled across the road and disappeared into somebody's backyard or up a drain-pipe. Every day the unlucky ones, the victims of speeding cars, would litter the streets like small wiry dachshunds. They lay on their sides and exposed their white bellies, their grey fur and thick rope-like tails. Above them hovered a cloud of black flies that probably mistook the rats for faeces.

Once at the booths Bertram found himself drinking beer after beer and just looking at people, many of whom he recognized, though he could no longer be sure of their names. He stood back and found some shadow against the wall of a freshly-painted booth, and then it dawned on him just how detached from the whole atmosphere he was feeling. He was not in any frame of mind to deal with conversations that would inevitably revolve around shared memories of events he would rather forget. As he drank on a mongrel-faced man, his knees thick and bruised, the calluses like scraps of heavy sandpaper, slumped down beside him. Bertram stared at the man's feet, the toes of which were chafed and unsightly, weblike through years of walking barefoot, and then Bertram's head began to spin. The man stammered, unable to flick the words off the end of his tongue, and Bertram realized that unless he made an immediate move for Sandy Bay he might end up supine beside his now horizontal friend.

Of the bus journey Bertram remembered little, except the unpleasant throbbing of his head, the insistent beat of the music, and the uncritical steering of the bus driver as they swung from one side of the road to the next. He had thought of chastising the driver, but he could feel only pity towards anyone stupid enough to give over a whole working life to driving a bus around an island with only one road. He spent most of the time staring out to sea, which in the darkness looked like a silky black cloth being stretched tight then slowly rippled by two invisible children.

Sandy Bay was quiet. A few penniless boys sat by the side of the road. They were the unlucky ones who had been unable to get a lift into town. From what Bertram could remember of the atmosphere down by the bayfront, they would have to wait a good few hours before they were likely to see their friends again. And then, as Bertram began to walk down Whitehall, it dawned on him that he could not return to his mother's house in this state. He decided to take another drink by Leslie Carter's so that he might feel confident his mother was asleep by the time he stumbled in.

Leslie Carter was looking up Whitehall. As Bertram saw him he began to feel embarrassed, but he was powerless to do anything about his lopsided gait. He entered the shop, but Mr Carter did not unfold himself from the counter until Bertram had finally settled on a stool. It was then that Mr Carter coughed, a loud consumptive cough that rumbled through his lungs before you heard it and after it had gone. He opened a beer and slid it across in front of his guest. Bertram smiled and took a quick drink, then he pushed his hand into his pocket and realized the situation he was in. He had no money. Mr Carter refolded himself over the counter. He did not appear to be expecting any money from Bertram, but Bertram felt that he had to say something. As he spoke he pushed his hand even deeper into his pocket.

'Mr Carter, it seems like I come out without any money.'

Mr Carter continued to look at whatever it was he had spent the most part of his life looking at.

'Well, you going anywhere?' he asked.

'Going anywhere when?' asked Bertram, his head now churning.

'You planning on leaving the island without paying me?'

'No', said Bertram, ''Course not. I going let you have the money first thing tomorrow. I let you have it tonight if you want.'

Mr Carter got up from the counter, took another bottle of beer from the freezer and snapped off the top. He placed it beside Bertram's still full bottle.

'Tomorrow is soon enough,' he said. 'If you say you going pay me then you going pay me, 150 per cent proof hangover or not.'

'Thank you,' said Bertram, feeling that such a brief and timid response to Mr Carter was almost insulting. But he had never heard such verbosity from Mr Carter, so he remained silent in the hope that he would say more. Mr Carter, however, had said all that he had to say, so Bertram sat and drank his two beers, glancing up just once to look at the bats sawing the night air with their busy flights.

When he finished, Bertram placed the two bottles together. He was attempting to draw Mr Carter's attention to the fact that he was going now, but Mr Carter turned to look at him as though asking what it was he was still doing fiddling around at the counter.

'Goodnight,' said Bertram.

Mr Carter gave him the briefest of nods, and Bertram stepped down into the street. He belched and stiffened in preparation, but the vomit did not come. Feeling as though he had a single iron handcuff around his temples, Bertram knew that the only alternative to staggering home and risking waking up his mother, was to go by Patsy. However, he was as unsure about his relationship to her as he was about his relationship to this island he still insisted on calling his home.

The slanting light fell through the window and struck Bertram in the face. He woke with a hammering in his head and panicked, unsure of the time. Then he took a look at the clock and saw that it had stopped. He got out of bed and tried in vain to touch his toes. It was already an inauspicious start to an auspicious day.

He stepped outside and repeated the ritual of a primitive wash by the side of the house. Today the dog growled at him, so he made ready to throw a kick at it. Then it stopped. Having washed he went back inside and took some clean clothes from one of the suitcases. Bertram guessed it must be after nine in the morning, and that his sleep had been a coma, his headache drink induced. He dressed, then peered around the corner into his mother's room, but she was still sleeping. Her cracked breathing sung out with a familiar and taunting unevenness, so he decided to leave.

As Bertram passed through the gate he noticed the two boys to whom he had given the ten-pence pieces. He pushed a hand into his trouser pocket, and then his mind switched back to last night: Bertram realized that he had left the house without money. He turned around, dashed back inside, and dug into his wallet for some notes. Then, remembering the two boys, he picked up some loose coins. Once back in the yard he gave the boys a dime each, and maybe because they recognized the money and knew exactly how little it could buy, they did not seem half as pleased as when he had given them the useless English money. Either way, he passed them by and made his way up the ghaut towards Leslie Carter's.

When he reached the shop Bertram crumpled a five-dollar bill on to the counter then moved to go. But Mr Carter's voice startled him.

'So what's this you're leaving here?'

'It's the money I owe you from last night.'

'So what happen, you win the Irish Sweepstake in England?'

Mr Carter opened his till and picked out a dollar bill. 'Two dollars a bottle.'

Bertram extended his hand and took the money. 'Well, maybe I can buy you a drink, then?'

'You, buy me a drink? Tell me, Mr Francis, when was the last time you saw me take liquor?'

Bertram remembered that Mr Carter never took strong drink, and he felt stupid for having suggested it.

'I can't let you treat me so without trying to show my gratitude.'

Mr Carter laughed, and Bertram shrugged his shoulders. Then Mr Carter began to attend to his shelves, so Bertram left the shop and walked quickly down Whitehall.

Bertram turned right into the alley that led to Patsy's house. When he reached her yard he went through the gate and walked straight up to the door. He knocked, but as he listened to the sound of his unanswered knocking he knew that he should not be doing this. The formality of it was ridiculous, so he did not bother to knock again. It briefly crossed his mind that Patsy might be entertaining a man, but he tried to banish this thought as soon as it appeared. He quickly left the yard and closed the gate behind him.

Once on Island Road Bertram had to wait for some time at the bus stop. As he did so he looked across at the hospital extension which, according to the posters, Princess Margaret would be opening later that same day. Children attired in their Sunday clothes were already milling around, and their mothers were struggling to keep them out of the dust and dirt. When the bus finally arrived, it was full of people trying to make their way to town so they might carry on the revelling they had left in the early hours of the morning. And as Bertram squeezed on, it became clear that he would have to make this journey to the capital standing up.

The bus turned a tight circle and pulled up at the bayfront. It was then that Bertram saw the merrymakers who had not managed to catch a night bus to the country. Most were sleeping, still curled up by the side of the road and unaware that the rays of the sun were now warming them. He got off the bus, looked at them, but knew that to stay drinking in this area was only going to depress him. He walked off in a different direction, and almost without knowing it Bertram found himself strolling out of Baytown towards the Royal Hotel. But, as he wandered along this country road, it dawned on him exactly how far he still had to trek, so he decided to stop and try to hitch a lift.

Up above the sun had now settled down to her daily task of scorching the dry earth a sandy brown, and all around the oppressive mid-morning air vibrated with an unrepentant vigour causing the small island world to shimmer. With an unmistakable rustle a mongoose darted its way out from the undergrowth, across the road, and towards a cluster of boys who were playing and shouting. Behind them the cane stood proud and ready to cut, and the sullen canecutters, splendid in their bright and dirty shirts, sprawled contentedly like dusty statues. When they moved it was like watching the birth of stone. In the fields a few laboured on. They hacked at the crop, looking like slaves of old, their bodies glued together with sweat. A woman stood by the roadside watching them, an empty tray balanced on her head. After a few minutes she turned and walked with a wide roll of her hips, moving as if a steel band were playing some barely audible rhythm along her spine. As she eased her way back towards Baytown the band played on.

Bertram was soon picked up by a man in a Suzuki jeep, whose spittle kept getting caught around the corners of his mouth, bubbling and bursting as he prattled on. It was an uncomfortable journey as the Japanese company had clearly put more effort into the styling of the exterior than the comfort of the interior. But the trip was short, and as he glanced up at the sun Bertram was reminded of how grateful he was for a lift of any kind.

The driver dropped him under the hotel canopy where another man, this one in an absurd brown uniform with yellow fringes, simultaneously opened the door to the jeep and held out his hand for a tip. Bertram stared at him, noticing that he already had too much change in his pockets for his jacket hung heavily, as if trying to slide off his shoulders and trip him as it concertinaed to his ankles. He tried not to laugh and simply pressed a quarter into the man's hand.

'Thank you, brother,' said the man. 'I'll buy us both a drink.'

It occurred to Bertram that he had probably short-changed him, but to have put his hand back into his pocket and given the man more money would have been an ugly admission. Avoiding his gaze Bertram marched quickly into the slick interior of the new Royal Hotel which seemed, at least to his amateurish eyes, as good as any he had ever seen in the West End of London.

The lobby was crammed with people, all of whom carried badges on their jackets or dresses which broadcast their name and country of origin. A group of local girls, who spoke foreign languages with differing degrees of proficiency, were acting as interpreter-chaperons to the predominantly male delegates. As Bertram looked around he could see that all was chaos, in keeping with a hotel lobby when a conference is taking place, although this conference had slightly more important political overtones. He pressed his way through the throng and took up a seat in the bar.

The lyricless whine that passed for music was playing so softly that it served only to irritate. Bertram looked around at those who sat before iced tumblers decorated with plastic sticks and spiked pineapple chunks, and he listened to the diplomatic whisper of their voices, the air drunk with conciliatory sentiments. A petite woman dressed in native batique surfaced beside his table.

'Can I take your order, sir?'

'I'll take a beer,' said Bertram, knowing that this would be the only beer he would drink in this hotel. Apart from himself and those serving, there were no other black people in the bar. To his immediate right sat a bald man with wispy brown hair that lightly covered the sides of his face, hair that suggested a bird's nest in preparation. His face was bloated, round and red, crinkly like an old tomato, and his loose flesh fell limply from his cheeks. Bertram read his badge, which proclaimed him head of the Canadian delegation. He watched as the man spoke through his cigar so it bobbled with every word. And away to his left, standing behind the reception desk, he could see the woman who appeared to be in charge of the hotel. She, too, was white, her accent when she raised her voice, unmistakably Scottish. Above her a large plaque on the wall confirmed that the hotel was in its third year of existence. It stood on ground that he, Jackson, Dominic, and others used to come and play on when they were children. In fact, it had not been possible to reach this part of the island by road. Only a boat or a long walk through the bush gave you access to it. But all that had changed, and now the hotel stood like a tropical Hilton with its own casino and video rooms, satellite dish and jacuzzis.

The small woman in native batique returned. She placed two wooden coasters before him, and put the beer on one and a chilled glass on the other. Then she tucked a neatly folded piece of paper under the edge of one of the coasters and turned to leave. As Bertram looked at the bill, he saw that it was totalled in American rather than Eastern Caribbean dollars, so he called the woman back. She came to him slowly, as though expecting his objection.

'You give me the bill in what currency?' he asked.

'In US dollars, sir.'

'You know where I am?' asked Bertram.

She stared directly at him. 'You're at the Royal Hotel bar, sir.'

'But not in America, right?'

She nodded and picked up the bill. He watched as she made some mental calculations, altered the figures, then placed it back down, its total now in the local currency. Bertram examined the bill then looked up at the woman.

'You know how long I've been away from this island?' The woman shook her head. 'Twenty years, and before I left here a single American dollar bill was as rare as snow from the sky.'

The woman looked as though she understood, but said nothing. She simply took Bertram's five-dollar bill and muttered, 'Thank you.' Acknowledging that he had perhaps been a little harsh, Bertram shouted after her.

'You can keep the change.'

The woman turned to look at him, but she cast him a look so ambiguous that Bertram hastily dropped his eyes to his beer. Then he left the bar and made his way out into the fresh air.

The grounds of the hotel featured two swimming-pools, six tennis courts, a golf course, and an artificial boating-lake. It was only when he saw the lake that he remembered the boy from the previous day. Bertram began to explore more purposefully, feeling that he now had a reason for being here.

He found Livingstone sitting under a tree with two other boys. The three of them were digging into a coconut they had obviously just cut open. Behind them was a red flag on the end of a tall pole, the thirteenth hole. A smiling Bertram walked towards the boys, hoping that Livingstone would recognize him.

'Still no badge,' began Livingstone. 'And before you ask me, I didn't see her yesterday. She didn't come back.'

'Well anyhow, thanks for waiting,' said Bertram.

'I didn't wait for long,' said the boy. 'I have a job to do as you can see.'

'You want to show me around your estate?'

'Sure,' said the boy. He got up and turned to his two friends. 'This here is Sidney.' A buck-toothed boy, who was as tall as Livingstone, got to his feet and held out a sweaty hand. Bertram shook it and smiled at Sidney.

'Eddie is my other workmate.'

Eddie, slightly smaller and stockier in shape, got to his feet and offered Bertram a similarly moist handshake.

'Well, all three of you can show me around.'

'Not much to see down here,' said Livingstone, two damp crescents of sweat soiling his otherwise spotless Chicago Bears tee-shirt. 'But maybe we take a walk up the hill from where you can see everything.'

Bertram followed as the three of them ambled off between the palms, and around the golfing greens. Then they started to climb up a steep and badly-trodden path.

'When you get to the top here,' said Livingstone, 'you

can see all the hotel grounds, and an aerial view of the hotel itself.'

Bertram nodded appreciatively, but he began to feel hot as the climb became harder. He stumbled and pricked his hand on a thorn, then he stopped for breath by the foot of a tree but they simply pressed on without him. As he saw the boys disappearing from view he realized he would have to follow or he would lose them altogether.

They were waiting for him at the summit, the three of them sitting like magistrates. Bertram slumped down beside Livingstone, unable to disguise the deep breaths he was having to take.

'You alright?' asked Livingstone. Sidney interrupted before Bertram could answer.

'Breathe slowly and you soon feel good again.'

He smiled a large toothy smile, then continued, 'We sometimes taking tourists up here and they find it real hard too. It's not just you, everyone don't like the climb but they dig the view.'

Bertram gazed down at the hotel, which from this height looked like a large greenhouse surrounded by the two blue squares of the pools, and the six green squares of the tennis-court complex. Behind the hotel the cars gleamed as the sun caught their waxed bodies.

'I think I better take a rest,' said Bertram.

'Well, you can see where I work now,' replied Livingstone. He stood up and slipped his harnessed sunglasses on to his face. 'We have to go so we check you later.' The others stood with him. 'You have your view so don't spoil it by rushing off. Not many people ever get this vantage point.'

And with that the three boys scampered off and left Bertram exhausted and perched on top of the hill. As they passed beneath the trees Bertram laughed. They were kind but wild, as he had been at their age. He leant back and let his hands form a soft-fingered cushion for his head, then he fell into a summery sleep.

Bertram woke suddenly. He glanced up and saw that the sunlight now fell slatted and pyramid-like, as if heaven were trying to highlight the sections of the island to be saved in a time of catastrophe. Then Bertram looked into the distance and watched the buggies that dashed between the hotel and the dunes, throwing up a small spray of dust as they did so. A thin line of palms fringed the beach, and beyond the palms the sea broke in parallel lines with a soft sigh he could hear even from this height. Back on land, the birds had stopped singing and the animals now sought shade under helplessly swollen rubbery green trees. The mid-afternoon battle had commenced, with only the hazy passage of an outsize cloud offering the briefest of relief. Bertram stood up and shook himself. He realized that he ought to try and make his way back to Baytown and perhaps pick up a drink.

Once there Bertram bought a beer and began to wander the streets. He passed Government House, where the uniformed man still stood by the gate trying to appear menacing. Bertram slowed and turned, then he walked back and stopped in front of the man. He looked contemptuously at the young guard's old machine-gun before speaking.

'I've come to see Jackson Clayton.'

The man looked into the distance.

'You have an appointment, sir?'

'You don't remember me?' asked Bertram in disbelief.

The man glanced down at the now empty bottle of beer that Bertram clutched, then again he looked away.

'You cannot see Minister Clayton without an appointment.'

'Well, I'm an old friend of his and I have to talk with him on some business.'

'Go and talk with the man at the window.'

Bertram knew the routine.

The man at the window sat with his feet up on the desk. Bertram knew he would have to begin again.

'I come to see Minister Jackson Clayton.'

Bertram felt it would be safer to offer some title, though it made him uneasy to have to go through this 'Minister' charade.

'You know what today is?' asked the man. Bertram nodded. The man went on. 'You have an appointment?'

Bertram shook his head. Then he realized that non-verbal answers would get him nowhere.

'I was thinking that maybe if he's in I could have a quick word and finish off some business we been talking about.'

'So you decided to just drop by?'

'It just so happened that I was passing.'

There was a short pause as Bertram registered that he had run into a brick wall.

'I didn't know what time it was so I thought I'd just try.' The man said nothing so Bertram went on. 'Well, is Minister Clayton in? If he is, maybe you could telephone his secretary and let her know that I've been remiss in calling like this, but I would like to see him.'

The man sucked his teeth then picked up the telephone.

'Yvonne, it's you? William Gumbs here.'

There was silence as Bertram first listened, then tried not to listen to what was being said. Then the man put down the receiver.

'Well, Minister Clayton is there but he's far too busy to see you.'

'I see,' said Bertram. 'Minister Clayton said that or his secretary?'

The man looked sternly at him. 'You didn't hear what I said, fellar?'

The street celebrations were in full swing as Bertram now began to amble down towards the harbour. He looked up at the row of new flags that fluttered above him, and for the first time he felt that the new design was absurd. The scrappy pieces of cloth looked as comically colourful as his mother's home. Most were draped on or around People's House, the rickety headquarters of the political party in opposition. A now-faded wooden sign above the door informed him that the party had been 'incorporated with the Mental and Manual Worker's Union in 1938'. A poster flapping loosely against the door advised him of last week's 'socio-economic' workshop.

TONIGHT THERE WILL BE A CANE-BREEDING
WORKSHOP ON HOW TO COUNTER-ATTACK AGAINST
SMUT DISEASE AND RUST DISEASE. WE BELIEVE
THAT SUCH AN INQUIRY WOULD BRING TO LIGHT
MUCH OF THE FILTH AND DIRT OF EXISTING
CONDITIONS UNDER WHICH THE MASSES LABOUR

Bertram walked on, and once at the bayfront he listened to the raised voices that stung the atmosphere with drink-infested chatter. These men listened to themselves talking, then burst out laughing and took another drink. But their conversations led nowhere. Their talk existed simply to kill time. Bertram leaned against a booth and ordered first one beer, then a second, and then a third. Then he noticed the now familiar debris around his feet, and this only served to depress him further. The heat was making Independence-ville smell sour, of too many bodies in a close space, so having finished his third beer Bertram walked across to the Ocean Front Bar where he found Denton's son sitting on the counter reading a comic.

'I don't see you in here for a couple of days,' began Lonnie. He scratched at an ear, which Bertram felt was unwise as it only drew attention to its magnitude.

'I've been busy.'

'Everybody's been busy. Every night we selling more beer in here than we done since my father died.'

'That's good.'

'Well,' said Lonnie thoughtfully, 'it's good on the money side, but not so good for me as I still can't seem to be able to afford any help.'

They heard the girl in the kitchen cracking out an icetray over the sink.

'She don't be much use to me,' said Lonnie, 'but I guess if you really want to make some money in this country you best butter up your backside with some bendover oil and point your arse towards New York.'

Bertram laughed and climbed up on to a bar stool.

'Or else get a Big Burger contract,' said Lonnie, 'or

sell the little Yankee mailboxes with a flag on them. We living on an island where the typists can't type, where we have power cuts all the time, the movies pirated on ZYZ still have the New Jersey logo on them, the sea has sewage accidently discharged into it, we have twenty-four-hour bars that close, and the roads still breaking an axle every day. And what is the response from the people with the money? The Rotary Club decide to donate a dustbin to every village, you can believe that? As a people we come like prostitutes just lifting up our skirts to anybody with cash, but before my mouth run off with me you better tell me what it is you want to drink.'

'I'll take a beer.'

Lonnie snapped the top off a bottle, then slid it across in front of Bertram.

'Cheers.'

'Cheers,' chorused Lonnie.

Bertram took a drink, but it was only as he lifted the bottle to his mouth for a second time that he realized Lonnie was mimicking his voice.

'You think I sound English, then?'

'Rather, old chap. Isn't that what you say?'

'That's what they say.'

Bertram took a drink and looked at Lonnie, hoping that they now understood each other. Lonnie smiled back.

'You expecting Jackson to pass by here today?' asked Bertram.

'You mean Jackson X?' Bertram looked puzzled. 'I hear that's what he used to call himself for a couple of years in the late 'sixties.'

'Jackson X?'

'Minister Jackson X is more regular than the sun.' Lonnie pushed back his grubby cuff and took a look at his watch. 'He soon be coming through. You shouldn't have to wait too long.'

'Good. Thanks.'

Bertram took another drink and noticed Lonnie staring at him.

'I think I'll take a seat at his table and wait for him over there,' suggested Bertram.

'You mean to try and give him a little surprise like before?'

'Something along those lines.'

Bertram threaded his way across the bar and sat at Jackson's table. As yet he had no idea what he would say to the minister, but he tried not to worry about this.

It was only when Bertram heard Jackson's voice that he realized he must have nodded off.

'I hear you come looking for me without an appointment.'

'I was looking for a man who used to be a friend.'

'I see,' said Jackson, moving around to sit opposite him. 'Well, when your friend is also a minister you can't expect to just come and see him like that.'

'How you mean?'

'You don't just pass by on your ministers and things in England, do you? You don't just happen to be passing Downing Street so you drop in for a quick word with the Cabinet?'

'I see,' said Bertram.

'Good, I'm glad you see for I was a little worried about you. Worried that maybe you lost all sense of perspective.'

'Maybe it's you who lost all sense of perspective?' retorted Bertram. Jackson looked sharply at him, but said nothing. Bertram glared back and realized he was already being drawn into a conversation unapologetically hostile in its intent. Then Lonnie appeared at their table.

'Just bring me a beer for now,' said Jackson. Lonnie turned to Bertram.

'You want a next beer too?'

Bertram nodded. Jackson waited until Lonnie had passed back across the bar before laughing.

'So you think I lost some sense of perspective?'

Bertram could feel the anger rising inside himself. 'I didn't say you lost it, I said you might have lost it. I was speculating.'

'Well, in that case let me pass on a little advice to you. Don't speculate so much. It don't suit your health.'

Lonnie returned and placed the two beers on the table. Jackson looked up at him. 'In about ten minutes bring me some curry goat.' Lonnie turned to Bertram, but Jackson took him by the arm. 'Just bring me a curry goat. I will be dining alone today.'

Lonnie said nothing as he turned away. Bertram tried hard not to let Jackson's words affect him, for he knew that this was exactly what Jackson was hoping might happen. He gulped a mouthful of beer, and then another, but his dry throat still swelled as though on fire.

'Up until today', said Jackson, 'it was a wise man on this island who never asked where he came from or who he was, but all that is about to change.'

'I don't know what you mean,' said Bertram.

'What I mean is I have work to do, the work of history. We must keep our conversation to the point.'

'Well, the point is', said Bertram, 'you were telling me that it might not suit my health to speculate too much.'

Again Jackson laughed. 'Let me put it more simply for you then. A boy like you leaves the island on a scholarship to England. It seems like you get nothing. Then you finally decide to come back. Apart from myself, nobody else who you left here really doing anything worthwhile so naturally you coming to see me.'

'I come to see you for I thought we were friends.'

Jackson snorted. 'You're clever, Bertram, but I'm not stupid.'

'I don't see how you mean?'

'We never did talk with each other before you left because for the last couple of weeks you too busy playing hurt about Patsy. You never did leave this island, my friend, so how it is you think you can suddenly arrive back and be so now? You didn't even write me. Maybe you forget how to write when you reach England for you didn't have Father Daniels to hold your hand.'

'Don't mock me, Jackson.'

'I'm not mocking you, I'm telling you the facts.'

'I come back here to try and make a new life for myself.'

'Well, I don't see nobody but yourself stopping you.'

'And you think it's that simple?'

'Well, thank God for that. At least you manage to get that much inside your head.'

Bertram sighed, and together they fell silent. Then Bertram decided to resume their conversation, for Jackson looked as though he was just waiting for his food.

'All I really want to know is if you're going to do anything to help me? I seem to remember you saying you would give me some advice.'

'I'll give you advice, but it might not be the same as helping you.'

'What advice?'

Jackson took a drink of beer, as though steadying himself. Bertram picked up his beer and did the same.

'The advice is I think you should go back to where you come from.'

Jackson waited for Bertram's protest, but as there was none he decided to continue.

'England is where you belong now. Things have changed too much for you to have any chance of fitting back, so why you don't return to the place where you know how the things are? You coming on here like a fool, just dropping by Government House and so on.'

Bertram looked at him, but still he said nothing.

'You English West Indians should just come back here to retire and sit in the sun. Don't waste your time trying to get into the fabric of the society for you're made of the wrong material for the modern Caribbean. You all do think too fast and too crazy, like we should welcome you back as lost brothers. Well, you may be brothers alright, but you lost for true for you let the Englishman fuck up your heads.'

Bertram looked at Jackson, but still he could find nothing to say. Like all politicians, Jackson's conversation was as straight as a motorway on which under-nourished ideas flashed past in both directions. This was a fact, easy to perceive, even simpler to comprehend. But what Bertram could not and would never be able to come to terms with, was the fact that this man had once been as close to him as his brother, Dominic. Like a fool he had expected more of Jackson, and he now despised himself, more than he despised the man in front of him, for having been so unforgivably naïve.

Eventually Lonnie arrived with the curry goat, and Bertram took this opportunity to stand up.

'Your food has arrived,' said Bertram.

Jackson did not reply for it was obvious that the food had arrived.

'So maybe I'll see you around then, Jackson.'

'Maybe you will, but I think you have certain things to deliberate upon.'

'You telling me how to run my life, Jackson?' Bertram now spoke boldly and freely.

'As long as you're on this island, Bertram, I will give you whatever advice I feel like giving to you.'

'Well, in future don't bother, you hear? I don't want it. Your advice is as meaningless as your title, for you still a small man to me. All that change is you're playing big.'

Bertram turned from Lonnie who was now a friend, and from the man of power who was now an enemy. He walked out into the street and down to the bayfront, where he bought and quickly disposed of a beer before going to sit on the end of the pier. Bertram stared out at the sister island, dull and moody in the background. In the foreground were the British gunboats, freshly anchored and ready to fire their independence salute. To their left the smaller fishing-boats of the soon to be liberated populace. He remembered the games they used to play as children. Their favourite was African

Crocodiles, which involved stripping some fool naked, usually him, and then dangling them over the end of the pier. Bertram could not swim so this game would generally end in his tears. As he looked out to sea it disturbed him that these memories should invade his mind at this particular moment, so he scrambled to his feet and decided to take a walk.

It seemed as though the noise and music was now growing with every hour. Bertram bought yet another beer and drifted up Fort Street towards Island Road. Once there he joined a group of people by the roadside, and he did not have to stand long before discovering what it was they were waiting for. As though from nowhere a car sped past. It was flanked on both sides by motor bikes, the new flag of independence flying from their handlebars. Princess Margaret's journey along the main thoroughfare was being made at what one could hardly call a regal pace. It was as though she was late for an appointment, and Bertram felt that someone had better tell her chauffeur to slow down otherwise he would soon drive her off the far end of the island. And then it was over, and the local cars were allowed back on to the road again, and the people began to disperse.

It was then that Bertram spotted Livingstone. He was sitting on the edge of the road by the petrol station with the other two boys, Eddie and Sidney. They waved as he walked towards them.

'I see you make it down the side of the hill,' said a grinning Livingstone, his wraparound sunglasses hiding his eyes.

'Not till late though. I fell asleep.'

'The climb tire you out?' asked the buck-toothed Sidney, a wicked smile creasing his face.

'Maybe,' Bertram laughed. 'You all not working?'

'No, we done now,' said Livingstone. 'But we must go back for the hotel having a beach-nic for the staff. We get some time off to come and look at the Princess before it start.'

'And what did you see?'

Livingstone sucked his teeth.

'A car belonging to the Governor, and a couple of stupid arses on motor bikes looking like they ready for the car to run them down.'

The boys stood up as Bertram started to laugh.

'Well, perhaps I see you all later,' said a hopeful Bertram. 'I'm going to take a lime down by Independence-ville tonight. You all going make it down there?'

They looked at each other, then Livingstone became their spokesman. 'I don't see why not. It's the night everyone been waiting for.'

'Good,' said Bertram. 'Maybe you all can teach me a few things about liming youth-style.'

It was their turn to laugh, and as they did so they turned and walked away. Bertram watched them disappear, then he began to wander back in the direction of the bayfront where he decided to buy one final beer before taking a bus back to Sandy Bay.

Patsy sat in her yard shelling peanuts. The breeze shimmered her dress and made it dance up and down her legs. Some of the papers from the previous day still lay on the ground by her feet. Then she glanced up and saw a dishevelled Bertram before her. He was looking over the gate as though he had never before seen anybody shelling peanuts. Patsy laughed to herself and went back to her chore.

'Bertram, you seem lost. You looking for something?'

'It's alright if I come in?' asked Bertram.

Patsy laughed openly now. 'Since when have you had to ask if you can come into my place?'

Bertram knew that this was all the answer he was going to get. He pushed open the gate and came and stood before her. There was nowhere to sit so he continued to stand, feeling like a spare piece of furniture.

'Bertram, you must be really drunk to be acting so damn foolish. Go inside the place and pick up a chair and come and sit down, nuh.'

Bertram obeyed and went through the door that was already waiting and ajar. Inside was just as he remembered, dark and sweet-smelling. A single candle tried to shed light into the corners of the room, but it made little impression. Bertram was fascinated by the fact that the tip of the flame was feathered with spiralling smoke that spun only inches before disappearing. Then he looked around and picked up a chair with legs so bowed it seemed as though it was squatting. As he lifted the chair, he caught the edge of a familiar and once-patterned rug. He rearranged it, but noticed that the small piece of carpet had aged badly and now oozed just the one sludge colour.

Bertram carried the chair out into the yard and placed it to the side of Patsy. He sat and watched her for a few moments, then spoke as though it was his turn to say something.

'I'm having a little trouble with my mother.'

Patsy laughed. 'You sound surprised.'

'I am surprised.' Bertram paused. 'I never in my life had any real kind of disagreement with my mother. I don't see why we should start now.'

Patsy stopped shelling her peanuts.

'Bertram, you're talking foolishness, and I can't believe a grown man like you don't realize so.'

'How you mean?' asked Bertram.

'You trying to tell me you think she have nothing to be upset about after you leave her and your brother for all this time. I'm surprised she let you back in the house.'

'Well, she tell me that she don't want me back in it no more.'

'I see, then you do have a problem.' Patsy returned to her peanuts. 'But then again you soon going be building a big house down by the beach, a house bigger than anyone ever built before, isn't it?'

Bertram was annoyed but he said nothing. Patsy twisted around so she now faced him, then she carried on.

'But that will be after you open up the black man's business that bound to make you come a millionaire in a few weeks at the most.'

'I can't see no joke,' said Bertram. He paused, then decided he had nothing to lose in unloading a few more of his problems while he still had somebody to share them with. 'And I went to see Jackson, but it don't seem like he's too interested in helping out an old friend.'

Again Patsy laughed, then she put the peanuts to one side.

'Bertram, you honestly think Jackson Clayton is interested in helping anybody else except himself? He don't have no time for small people.'

'You still seeing Jackson?' asked Bertram, embarrassed that he should have phrased his enquiry so bluntly. Patsy sucked her teeth.

'I look like the woman of a government minister to you?'

Bertram looked away, now realizing the full stupidity of his question. For twenty years he had suffered the dull ache of his failed relationship with Patsy. A constant torment had been his recurrent visions of Jackson passing his rough hands across her body, then entering her with the sensitivity of an unoiled piston. He could not help but ask.

'I stopped seeing Jackson even before you left to go to England. You didn't realize that?'

'No,' said Bertram, shaking his head.

'You mean you spent all this time thinking Jackson and me still having a thing?'

'I wasn't sure.'

Patsy put a hand on Bertram's knee, as though comforting a slightly simple child.

'I could have told you that Jackson isn't going to help you. He probably still sees you as some kind of rival, for he never really forgave you for capturing the scholarship and stealing his little bit of cricket thunder from him.'

'Well, I don't see why that can't just fall into the past now,' said Bertram. 'What is done is done.'

'You really feel so?' said Patsy. 'Nothing in this place ever truly falls into the past. It's all here in the present for we too small a country to have a past.'

Bertram looked at her, and Patsy stared back.

'Tell me, Bertram, what else it is you didn't realize? You know that Father Daniels die?'

Bertram shook his head.

'Well, he did die in church so at least he went off well dressed for the next world.'

Bertram lowered his eyes and kicked at an empty peanut shell.

'And I suppose nobody tell you about Dominic until you reach back here?'

Again Bertram shook his head.

'Well, I don't think you could have altered the situation so don't let your mother trouble your head on that front. The two of them mash up when your mother catch him in her house winding with a next man's wife. So Dominic left to stay up town where he start to hit the liquor so hard people begin calling him Bacchus Francis. He almost certainly fall out of the factory and under the car so don't feel no guilt, you hear me. It would have happened whether you here or not, for when a man is destined to take up the drink profession then that is it and there's nothing nobody can do.'

Patsy paused and looked at Bertram, then she shrugged her shoulders and carried on.

'And after your mother find him checking the woman, she take to her bed and I can't believe she move out of it since.'

'But it's true that they never catch anyone for Dominic's death?' asked Bertram.

'The police here never catch anyone for anything for they too busy chasing women.'

There was another pause, then Bertram looked at Patsy.

'And what about you now?' he asked.

'What about me?' said Patsy. 'I'm an unmarried woman. A mule, as the more charming of the men around these parts insist on calling me.'

'You never have any children?'

Again Patsy laughed. 'Maybe it's best we don't talk about it, Bertram.'

'Why not?'

'Because all I can remember is that the only time I start to get seriously big in front my auntie just take one look at me and tell me I'm a picked fruit rotting. Nobody ever hurt me so much, either before or since.'

'I see.' Bertram paused, then pressed on.

'Well, what happened to the child and who is the father?'

'I was four months a lover and nineteen years a mother, that does sound fair to you?'

'I don't think there's much in life that is fair to any of us.'

'I can promise you,' said Patsy, 'you don't need to go to England to find that out.'

They were silent, then Bertram sighed and spoke again.

'So you don't want to answer my question about the child?'

Patsy took his hand and looked into his face.

'Bertram, I answered you. Later on, maybe tomorrow, I'll answer you again in a more straight manner.'

Again they were both silent. Then Bertram stood up, feeling that perhaps he was wasting her time.

'I better go now.'

'And exactly where it is you planning on going to?'

Bertram looked at her, wishing she had not asked him such a direct question for he had no place to go. But he was desperate that he should not appear either lost or rootless on his own island.

'Maybe I'll take a walk around the village and see if I bump into anyone.'

'You meet anyone as yet?'

'I see people but I'm not so sure that it's them. I don't like to ask just in case I'm wrong.'

Patsy laughed. 'This place really got you acting strange.'

'Well, I suppose a part of the truth is that after the Dominic thing I've not wanted to talk with people in case I have to deal with anything else I don't want to know about.'

'Anything like what?'

'I don't know, Patsy.'

Patsy stared hard at Bertram, but he turned away, clearly wishing to avoid any further questioning.

'Perhaps I'll come by and see you later?'

'You know where I live.'

'Yes, I know where you live.'

Bertram remained standing, but he displayed no signs of imminent departure. Patsy got up and walked away from him and into the house. Then, behind his eyes, Bertram could feel water rising. He pulled a handkerchief from his pocket and blew his nose. Then he blinked vigorously as a double precaution.

'You coming in or what?' shouted Patsy.

Bertram looked around in case anyone had either

heard Patsy shout, or was secretly witnessing his misery.

'You want me to come in?' asked Bertram, his voice transcending its normal pitch.

Patsy stepped back into the yard and stood before him.

'Bertram Francis, you want me to drag you in here?'

Bertram followed her inside the house and sat at the foot of the bed. He kicked idly at a ball of dust and knotted, then unknotted his fingers. He could feel her eyes upon him.

'Bertram, I don't have no man so why you can't just relax.'

He looked at her. With a single lick Patsy made her lips sensual.

'You have any plans for the rest of the day?' she asked.

'I don't have no plans to talk about, apart from going back to town for the celebrations tonight. You coming?'

'What it is they celebrating?'

'You know that tonight is the independence.'

'I know, and you think that is something to celebrate?'

'It's part of the reason why I come back.'

'You want to lie down with me?'

Something struck Bertram. Patsy's dress was riding up and exposing her fleshy thighs. He felt a stirring in his groin and against his will his penis leapt tall.

'I can't just lie down with you after all this time.'

'You mean you frightened to?'

Bertram did not want to have to admit to this. 'We both possibly a bit too old for such business,' he suggested.

'Speak for yourself,' laughed Patsy. She moved her face into the candlelight so that Bertram might read it better. 'Maybe you can convince yourself it's some kind of private celebration.'

'Maybe I can.'

Bertram leaned over and ran his hands down the side of her smooth oval face. Then he blew softly into her ear unsure if he was putting out, but hopeful that he might be starting, a fire.

'Maybe I can,' he said again.

Bertram put his lips to hers and pressed. Then he opened their mouths and felt her hot tongue begin to flick over and around the edges of his teeth. Patsy reached down, and Bertram felt himself swell and thicken in her fist. She leaned back, slipped off her pants, and eventually she encouraged first one, then a second, then countless intrusions into her body. Some time later Bertram shuddered. His body stiffened, its interior framework collapsed, and all his structural and emotional strength was drained away as if her soft female hand had wrenched out the plug of his masculinity.

When Bertram woke up they were teaspooned together, a thin film of sweat both holding and dividing them. Somewhere in a neighbouring house he could hear the ticking of a clock that matched the beat of his heart. He listened and tried to fight the tiredness that was still heavy upon him. Then Patsy stirred and turned to face him, her nose soft and flared like a brown flower. She kissed him, a morning kiss lightly sealed with the mutual guilt of bad breath, then her head made a pillow of his shoulder and she nuzzled up against his bristled cheeks. Patsy closed her eyes, and Bertram waited until he was sure she was asleep before he slid from the bed. Once around the back of the house, Bertram found that his penis was once again erect. He tried to coax it back into a more manageable position so that he might produce a downward curve of spent water, as opposed to a skyward parabola. And having done so, and shaken it dry, he returned to bed.

It was dark when Bertram awoke. He discovered himself alone in the bed, and as he looked up he saw Patsy standing by the small table and exposing her flaccid breasts. She wiped some sleep from her body with a damp towel, then she hung the towel back on the wall and moved across to the stove. Once there she poured some water into a large pot.

Bertram propped himself up on one elbow.

'What time is it?'

'I don't know,' said Patsy, 'but you have plenty of time for the celebrations don't really going to start until midnight.'

'I know, but it might be midnight.'

'I don't think so,' said a confident Patsy. 'You have time.' She returned to her cooking. 'Tell me, who it is feeding and looking after your mother?'

'Mrs Sutton, though she don't look that much better than Mummy.'

Patsy glanced at him, but Bertram looked away guiltily.

'You know, I wanted to do something for your mother,' said Patsy, 'but I just couldn't seem to find a way of approaching her. It seems like a bad excuse to you?'

'I understand,' said Bertram.

He swung his naked body out from under the sheet and sat on the edge of the bed. Patsy, a large spoon in her hand, stopped stirring and stared brazenly at him. Her eyes made him feel uneasily aware of his genitals, which hung loose and foolish.

'You're a good-looking man, Bertram Francis. Still a little scrawny around the waist, and somewhat thin in the face, but you still look to me like a handsome man. I'm just surprised no English girl didn't snatch you up as yet.'

Bertram reached for his trousers, which lay on the floor. Then he watched, as again Patsy's mind swung and this time curved more purposefully in the direction of England.

'Well,' she said, 'tell me, any English girl snap you up as yet?'

This time he knew he would have to answer.

'I'm not married, if that's what you mean.'

'That's not what I mean,' she said. 'If I'd have meant that I would have said so.'

Bertram looked closely at Patsy's face. She still had strong graceful lines, and perfectly vaulted eyebrows. Her beauty, and her strangeness of spirit were both still evident, but now that he was older Bertram could see other virtues in Patsy, though diplomacy could never be counted among them.

'I have somebody in England who is maybe waiting for me to come back, but I think it's just about finish.'

'You're not sure if it's finished?'

Bertram tried to think of how best he might explain, but every time he formulated a sentence that could lead him into some kind of clarification of his life in England, his thoughts became too complex and he withdrew. In the end he spoke plainly, his sense of resignation pricking every word.

'If you want me to just say everything I will.' He paused. Patsy said nothing so he went on. 'But the truth is I don't want you to make me do so. At least not just now, for I know it will come out upside down.'

'I don't want you to have to explain anything you don't feel like explaining.'

'Thank you,' said a grateful Bertram.

Patsy watched as he finished getting dressed. Then she began to serve his meal.

'But tell me one thing,' she said. 'You leave any children over there?'

Again Bertram was shocked by the boldness of her questioning. As he took his place at the table she touched his arm and smiled. 'Don't answer, Bertram. Seems like a wind must have blown through your head and filled it full of confusion.'

'I can't help it,' said Bertram. 'Things still messed up in my mind. Last night, for instance, I find myself dreaming about fog.'

'About what?' asked Patsy.

'About the fog they had in England when I first arrived. English fog always used to seem to me like a grey-white blanket that would rip as easily as water, yet it was as thick as solidified coconut milk. It used to fascinate me, you know. In those first few months when I arrived in England everything was either fascinating or frustrating or both. Things sometimes difficult, but I have the scholarship money and if you have money in England you can get by.' He paused. 'Anyhow, I didn't want to be no lawyer so I used to ask myself why the hell I should study so hard.'

'Then why the hell did you go?' asked Patsy.

'I had to go, I captured the scholarship.' He paused. 'After two years they tell me I must leave the college so I take a job. Then I take a next one and so on, until my time just slide away from me. I know it don't sound too impressive, but there's plenty more just like me still in England. People who went there for five years, then one morning they wake up with grey hair and wonder what happened. Well, what happened is called a life, and it just passes away from you unless you do something about it and discipline yourself.'

'And now you're back,' said Patsy.

'And now I'm back.' Bertram paused. 'But perhaps I come back too late.'

'Too late for who, or what? All I know about that place is from the cricket reports, but it seems to me like it's always raining, and I know for sure that the people don't be no good.'

Bertram squeezed Patsy's hand and drifted into the miasma of his jumbled memories. He knew that to her, like most people who had never left the island, Europeans were like hurricanes, unpredictable, always causing trouble, always talked about, a natural disaster it was impossible to insure against. His mind sailed back to those first few months in England, but all he could recall was the excitement of being able to begin his life anew, and the frustration of trying to understand a people who showed no interest in understanding him. His gradual descent to the point where he stopped sipping at life's experience and started to swallow it in great greedy mouthfuls had been swift. After two or three weeks he had known that perhaps he would one day have to return home empty-handed. In the meantime he had felt compelled to relinquish his family photographs, for they had become a reminder of loneliness as opposed to a temporary cure. And then, as he learned to relax into wasteful English gluttony, they became something more sinister: evidence of guilt. His only regret had been that he did not have a photograph of Patsy to jettison.

Patsy kissed him on the forehead and watched as he began to eat. Eventually the fork clattered against the plate. Bertram scratched back the chair and stretched. Then Patsy spoke quietly.

'So you don't know if you're going back to England?'

Bertram did not look up at her, as though ashamed of his own indecision.

'I haven't made up my mind.'

'I'm not rushing you out of my home.'

'I know and appreciate that.' He paused. 'I really have nothing to go back to in England.'

'Nothing?'

'Nothing except a place and a people I know and don't care much for.'

'You don't feel at home there?'

'But I . . .' he paused. Patsy took his hand and he found the confidence to continue. 'But', he said, 'I don't yet feel at home back here either.' He loosened himself from her grip and stood. 'Maybe I better go now.'

Patsy looked up at him. The moon caught the slight lustre on his face. 'You coming back here again tonight?'

Bertram felt coy. 'You want me to?'

'You think I would ask if I didn't want you to?'

'It will be late.'

'Well, you know where the door is.'

Bertram kissed her and turned to leave. Patsy stood and followed him out into the yard. Then she watched as he passed through the gate and down the small alley towards Whitehall.

The bus hurtled in the direction of the capital as though being sucked in by the excitement of what was about to happen. Once in Baytown Bertram tried to make his way quickly to the park, but like a bent pipe the streets were clogged with latecomers. Line upon line of cars jammed every road and junction, but after much tedious waiting the people and vehicles began to thin out.

When he arrived at Stanley Park, Bertram craned his neck and looked down at the countless rows of assembled guests. Their innumerable heads looked like a huge basket full of miniature moons, and their moon-faces were painted with a dreamlike benevolent austerity. Then Bertram looked beyond them and saw that the platforms for the dignitaries had been constructed where the cricket square usually was. But, to his left and to his right, above, below and around him were the people, their faces gleaming, the tops of their heads dry and brittle, though some were slicked and greasy for this special occasion.

Bertram was late and the state service already under way. Then, barely a few minutes after his arrival, he listened as the Doctor delivered the climactic line of his speech.

'I have squatted three hundred and fifty years in another man's house, now that house is mine own!'

The applause was thunderous, and Bertram watched the new flag slide up the pole and cross the old one slithering down. In the distance he heard the cracked report as the guns of the British Royal Navy fired their salute, and overhead a cloud of doves flew in all directions, glad to have escaped their independence baskets. As the church clock struck midnight, and the cheering and celebratory noises grew even louder, Bertram heard raindrops beginning to slap against the leaves of the trees above him. Then as the wheels of history turned, and Mount Misery became Mount Freedom, and Pall Mall Square became Independence Square (although the island had decided to keep its old colonial name), someone punched a hole in the sky and everybody ran for cover as the rain broke through. As they did so the police band started to play the new national anthem in G major like the old British one, but they struggled to find the notes to this new tune. Bertram listened to their waterlogged and unmusical rendering of what seemed an otherwise pleasant composition, but before the band could rescue the anthem the heavens opened wide. The musicians now ran for cover, and all around the umbrellas bloomed like flowers, and the sharp bullets of rain joined the sky to the earth.

Bertram ran quickly but aimlessly, and as he did so he noticed that the dignitaries now had little choice but to mix with the ordinary people in this teeming confusion.

He recognized the tall figure of a radical leader from a neighbouring island. He was flanked by gunmen, their jackets bulging. And then he saw a woman leader popularly known as the Iron Woman of the Caribbean. Her umbrella had been peeled inside out by the high wind, and a civil servant nobly held his coat above her head. As she turned, presumably to thank him, Bertram noticed that her upper plate dropped and kissed its partner. A simple pursing of the lips retrieved the situation.

Gradually the drumroll of rain on the car roofs eased to a pitter-patter, and the cars rubbered along in the wet throwing up thin sheets of water. Bertram found himself in a steady stream of people pouring down towards Independence-ville, where the wooden booths were now dazzlingly lit. He prepared himself, ready to drink until dawn on this first day of a new era in his island's history.

Having bought a beer, Bertram stood to one side and looked around himself. He saw Jackson, who noticed him but simply stared back as though Bertram was an early-morning apparition. And beyond Jackson, he saw Livingstone and his friends. He wanted to go across and say something to them, but they were young people occupied with their own revelry. If they had any sense they would be chasing girls and filling themselves with more drink. The idea of wasting their time on an old man from England was ridiculous. What seemed even more ridiculous was that Bertram had ever imagined they would want to. He laughed and took a drink, knowing that neither he nor Dominic would ever have entertained such an idea. Then Bertram turned from the boys and went quickly to buy another beer. He felt distressed that he had allowed himself to think of Dominic in terms of women and drink, but the storm that now raged inside of his head could only be quelled by solitude. Bertram took his fresh beer and went to sit on the end of the pier.

Four hours passed before the sun appeared on the horizon. Bertram leaned forward, tossed his empty beer bottle into the sea, then stood up. Dominic had crept from all corners of his mind and occupied the centre. By means of gentle persuasion Bertram had encouraged him to retreat again, promising him that a dialogue would be re-established once he had found himself. And now Bertram drifted away from the quietude of the pier and the turmoil of Independence-ville, and he moved off in the direction of Sandy Bay having decided to walk back the six miles looking, remembering, and planning.

As he passed out of Baytown, Bertram saw an old man sitting by the side of the road, his mouth open as if ready to speak. But he said nothing. Bertram recognized him as Buddy, a man who was already a legend in his own lifetime. He used to be a cane cutter, but many years ago he had decided that the dividing line between his profession and that of a tramp was slim enough for him to hang up his machete. His first action was to walk from Sandy Bay to Baytown in his only suit (a suit which had been his father's before him), and present himself at the Carib Creole, the only establishment on the island that was then brazen enough to appropriate the name restaurant. He ordered and disposed of a large and expensive meal, then he calmly asked the waiter to put his bill on the Governor's account. Buddy's place in Sandy Bay folklore was secure.

Bertram looked at him as he cowered by the side of the road, his feet unshod and each toe the length and breadth of his big toe. His trousers were frayed at the bottom as well as at the top, his shirt, discoloured with sweat, hung open and dirty from his hunched shoulders. But his face told the grimmest story. His few remaining teeth formed a yellow portcullis, and his matted hair resembled a grey scouring-pad. Bertram remembered him as a man who, if he talked for long enough, you would be happy to give a cigarette to, not in the hope that he might go away, but because of the pleasure of his anecdotes. But this morning he said nothing. Behind him the deep green fields were spread out like a woollen blanket. And beyond the fields the morning light made a jewelled mirror of the sea. For Bertram this dawn, usually the loneliest part of the day, was both fuller and more disturbing than any he had ever experienced. He contemplated the abandoned and crumbling sugar mills, modest, almost discreet reminders of a troubled and bloody history. Unsure of what they represented, nobody had ever bothered to demolish them. Instead they had been content to see them either collapse into disrepair, or be converted into centrepieces for hotel complexes. Bertram rambled past these historical ruins, and then he pressed on purposefully.

He tried hard to imagine how he might cope, were he to make peace with his own mediocrity and settle back on the island. And then he glanced upward. He saw a man who, at this time of the morning and considering what was happening in Baytown, appeared unreal. The man was threading wires from telegraph pole to telegraph pole, as though trying to stitch together the island's villages with one huge loop. Then Bertram remembered. That evening the people would receive their first cable television pictures, live and direct from the United States. Bertram waved courteously to the man and turned away. Then he spat. He ground the spittle into the Tarmac with the tip of his shoe. And then he walked on and wondered if later this same day he should ask Mrs Sutton how he might help his mother.

St Kitts, 20 June 1985